T3-BNK-891

ORGANISING MUSIC IN LIBRARIES

VOLUME TWO

Cataloguing

ORGANISING MUSIC IN LIBRARIES

VOLUME TWO

Cataloguing

BRIAN REDFERN

CLIVE BINGLEY
LONDON

LINNET BOOKS
HAMDEN · CONN

FIRST PUBLISHED 1966
THIS REVISED AND REWRITTEN EDITION PUBLISHED 1979
BY CLIVE BINGLEY LTD
1-19 NEW OXFORD STREET LONDON WC1
SIMULTANEOUSLY PUBLISHED IN THE USA BY LINNET BOOKS
995 SHERMAN AVENUE HAMDEN CONNECTICUT 06514
SET IN 10 ON 12 POINT PRESS ROMAN BY ALLSET
PRINTED AND BOUND IN THE UK BY REDWOOD BURN LTD
TROWBRIDGE AND ESHER

BINGLEY ISBN: 0-85157-261-8
LINNET ISBN: 0-208-01678-3

Library of Congress Cataloging in Publication Data

Redfern, Brian L
Organising music in libraries.

Bibliography: p.
CONTENTS: v. 1. Arrangement and classification. —v. 2. Cataloguing.
1. Music libraries. 2. Classification—Music. 3. Cataloging of music. 4. Cataloging of phonorecords. I. Title.
ML111.R4 1978 025.3'4'8 78-819
ISBN 0-208-01678-3

CONTENTS

PREFACE

THIS VOLUME completes the revised edition of *Organising music in libraries* somewhat later than predicted in volume one. This is mainly due to the later-than-expected appearance of the second edition of the *Anglo-American cataloguing rules.* It has been a difficult task to complete a comparative survey of that code and the IAML codes in the first three months of 1979, and I am very conscious that the final product is not as polished as I would like it to be. Nevertheless I respect the needs of my publishers to keep to their programme and it will hopefully prove useful to have some comment on the treatment of music by the new rules so soon after their publication.

I hope the opportunity for a further revision will occur once use of AACR 2 has settled down, and I would welcome comment from anyone who is interested, particularly practising cataloguers. All communications should be sent to me at the Polytechnic of North London and will be acknowledged.

Many people have contributed to my knowledge already. In particular I would like to thank the other members of the Sub-Committee of the United Kingdom Branch of the International Association of Music Libraries on Revisions to AACR (Richard Andrewes, Clifford Bartlett, Malcolm Jones, Miriam Miller and Patrick Mills), and my colleagues Antony Croghan, Eddie Garrett and Ellen Gredley for their help and stimulating ideas, even if I have not always agreed with all of them all of the time! I would finally like to thank Margaret, my wife, for enduring with so much patience the presence of a zombie-like creature in her home during a long hard winter. I know I have talked of little else but cataloguing codes in that time.

Brian Redfern, Principal Lecturer
School of Librarianship
The Polytechnic of North London
207-225 Essex Road
London N1 3PN, UK

ACKNOWLEDGEMENTS

GRATEFUL acknowledgement is made to the following publishers for permission to quote from their publications. Library Association : *Anglo-American cataloguing rules, Cutter's rules for a dictionary catalog.* C R Peters : International Association of Music Libraries' *Code international de catalogage de la musique* vols 1-4. International Federation of Library Associations : various ISBD's as listed in the introduction. Heinemann : *Harvard dictionary of music*, lst edition. Oxford University Press : *The structure of music* by R O Morris. The BBC Music Library : Instrumentation formula (draft) for the *Catalogue of the orchestral library*. The Music Bibliography Group : *Music and the Marc format.* International Association of Music Libraries (UK Branch) : *Union catalogue of orchestral scores and parts.* Richard Andrewes of the Pendlebury Music Library, Cambridge for permission to cite filing titles procedure : 'Procedure for formation of uniform titles'.

GLOSSARY

MANY OF the terms used in this volume are defined in the codes etc which are discussed. The definitions of some terms vary between codes, but in referring to a particular code or standard the definitions used within it must be accepted, of course, if the rules are to make sense. The terms below are either general in application or used in a special sense in this book. Some have been repeated from volume one for convenience.

Altus, Cantus, Tenor: terms defining the pitch of voices in early music.

Entry: a record of a bibliographical item in a catalogue or list. Sometimes confined to the heading for such a record.

Gesellschaft (German): society, company.

Literature: books about music.

Music: scores.

Passepartout: title page listing all the works of a composer in a series with the one contained in the volume to hand indicated.

Plate number: serial number given to each work by a music publisher and usually found at the foot of each page of the score.

Provenance: the history of a manuscript, particularly showing successive owners.

Score: a musical work in manuscript or printed form, generally used for works for two or more performers. A *full score* is a complete score, containing all the parts, instrumental and/or vocal, fully set out. A *miniature score* is a reduction of a full score. A *vocal score* consists of the original vocal parts with a reduction for keyboard of the orchestral parts.

ABBREVIATIONS

AACR 1 & 2	*Anglo American Cataloguing Rules* lst and 2nd editions (1967 & 1978).
BCM	*British Catalogue of Music* *or* the classification by which it is arranged.
BLCMP	Co-operative computer based cataloguing service, headquarters at Birmingham.
BNB	*British National Bibliography*.
DC	Dewey Decimal Classification.
LC	Library of Congress *or* its classification.
Lancet	Library Association and National Council for Educational Technology. *Non book materials cataloguing rules*.
IAML 1, 2, 3, 4, 5	International Association of Music Libraries. International cataloguing code for music. 5 vols. For details see p 12.
ISBD	International Standard Bibliographic Description. CM = Cartographic materials, G = General, M = Monographs, NBM = Non Book Materials, PM = Printed Music.
RISM	*Répertoire international des sources musicales.*

INTRODUCTION

THIS PROVIDES a brief, mainly factual, introduction to the cataloguing codes and international standards, the comparative study of which forms the main part of the book. All of them are basically concerned with problems of author/title headings and description. It cannot be too strongly emphasised that this book is not a cataloguing code. It is essential in fact to have copies of the relevant codes available for consultation, as reference is constantly made to the rules on the assumption that the reader is able to turn to them.

Anglo-American catalogue rules 2nd ed Library Association, 1978 (AACR 2).

The most important point to realize about this edition is that it represents a major change in layout from that of the first edition. Not only do the rules on description come first this time, but also, within each section of the whole code, whenever appropriate, the rules for special materials follow general rules applicable to all types of publication. Thus chapter 25 (Uniform titles) begins with a group of general rules and follows with special rules for composite manuscripts and manuscript groups, incunabula, legal materials, sacred scriptures, liturgical works, official papal communications and music.

The method of working has to be, always, to examine both the general and special rules in a particular chapter or section. It is impossible to catalogue music properly without consulting the general rules *at all times*. When the rules for music contradict the general rules, the former are to be used, but usually the special rules are interpretations of the general rules for the particular kind of material under consideration. This means that the cataloguer has to become very familiar with the layout of the code if it is to be used properly. The system of numbering the rules is very different from that used in AACR 1 and does not assist those accustomed to the first edition. The point is not used decimally, as has been the practice in many other publications including IAML 3. This rules 25.25 and 25.26 do not follow 25.2 and precede 25.3, but are arranged in arithmetical sequence under 25 ie 25.1 to 25.9, 25.10 to 25.19 etc. To anyone used to decimal notation this is confusing at first, but familiarity brings recognition of the effectiveness of the method, especially in view of the complexity of the material being organized.

The basic structure of the code is very simple. Part I covers description, Part II headings, uniform titles and references. Appendices cover Capitalization, Abbreviations, Numerals and Glossary. The glossary has some very unsatisfactory definitions of musical terms. For example, it defines *Score* as 'A series of staves . . .', but does not define *staves*. Anyone who knows what a stave is must surely know what a score is. In fairness AACR 2 enters a very confused world here, as a perusal of a number of music dictionaries has revealed. It does not help to solve any of the confusions by its definitions of close score, condensed score, conductor's score and short score. On the contrary it tends to add to them. For further comment on this see below under IAML 3 (p 14) and the glossary of this book.

AACR 2 is very clearly based on the International standards for bibliographical description (ISBDs), perhaps less obviously on the *Paris principles* resulting from the International Conference on Cataloguing Principles held in Paris in 1961, although it has moved much more closely to the latter than had AACR 1. It is also a code very much designed for use with computers.

Code international de catalogage de la musique. International Association of Music Libraries–International Cataloguing Code Commission. C F Peters, 1957-   . 5 volumes.

The individual volumes are as follows:

1 *The author catalog of published music* by Franz Grasberger, 1957 (IAML 1). This is a study of the problems and principles of producing a catalogue of music. It is not strictly a code and cannot be used as such, although solutions to the various problems raised are suggested. It is, however, a very useful comparative study and contains a number of examples of title pages with reproductions of entries made for them by some of the most famous music libraries in the world.

2 *Limited code* compiled by Yvette Fédoroff, 1961 (IAML 2). This volume is designed for use particularly by cataloguers without a knowledge of music, and particularly for use in music libraries forming

part of a more general collection but separated from it. As these aims imply, it does not offer the fullest cataloguing but does have helpful suggestions on how a catalogue may be effectively produced without supplying the fullest details. It has appendices on the limited treatment of manuscripts, brief rules for establishing conventional (uniform) titles and a plan for the systematic classification of a subject catalogue. It draws attention to continental practice in a number of places and some of the solutions proposed throw fresh light on old problems.

3 *Rules for full cataloging* compiled by Virginia Cunningham, 1971 (IAML 3) has the following stated aims and principles:

Purposes

1 To serve as a basic cataloguing guide for libraries and other institutions.
2 To facilitate the production of international and national bibliographies and catalogs.
3 To promote the development of cooperative cataloging arrangements among libraries and other institutions.
3 To facilitate the exchange of information among libraries, institutions, and international organizations.

Principles

1 The rules will reflect developments in international cataloging in other fields insofar as possible.
2 The rules are intended to produce entries that meet the requirements of research libraries and specialized collections, and to provide all the approaches to material that libraries need for their users.
3 The entries will include all the information about the music required by the musician, whether he is a performer, scholar, or amateur.

This is the IAML volume which is most frequently compared with AACR 2 in the following pages. Like that code it does not attempt to cover classification (ie shelf arrangement) or subject headings, in contrast with IAML 2 which does give guidance on these areas. Unlike AACR 2 it does not have rules on forms of names 'because forms of names should conform to standards accepted for the cataloging of books'. More than IAML 2 it is concerned to establish international standards for cataloguing music, to enable the free interchange of information between countries. Appendix 1 provides a number of useful examples which supplement those given under the actual rules. Appendix 2 is a glossary of terms compiled in English by Meredith

Moon, with translated lists in French and German. Appendix 3 is a list of recognized abbreviations for thematic catalogues. The glossary of terms is as unsatisfactory as that in AACR 2 and seems to have been the source of some of the confusions there. It was surely unsatisfactory also to base the German and French lists on the English one. There needs to be an international standard for definition of musical terms used in bibliographies and catalogues, but this will not be easy to achieve. Nevertheless IAML 3 is an invaluable cataloguing guide.

4 *Rules for cataloging music manuscripts* compiled by Marie Louise Gollner, 1975 (IAML 4). There is little to say about this code, which is discussed separately in the chapter on description (p 83). As the only available published code on its subject it is an essential tool for any cataloguer of music manuscripts. It has an appendix of examples which supplements those given with the rules.

5 *Rules for cataloging sound recordings*. Not yet published (IAML 5).

Even if cataloguers in the English speaking world are committed to the use of AACR 2, they will find the IAML codes helpful aids for cataloguing music. They represent the cataloguing experience of many countries and cannot be ignored as sources of guidance and help.

International standard bibliographic descriptions. International Federation of Library Associations, 1974- . These are the results of several years of hard work by members of the IFLA.

Their basic purpose is clearly stated in the preliminary notes to ISBD (G):

> The primary purpose of the International Standard Bibliographic Descriptions (ISBDs) is to aid international communication of bibliographic information by (i) making records from different sources interchangeable, so that records produced in one country can be accepted easily in library catalogues or other bibliographic lists in any other country; (ii) assisting in the interpretation of records across language barriers, so that records produced for users of one language can be interpreted by users of other languages; and (iii) assisting in the conversion of bibliographic records to machine readable form . . .
>
> . . . The description resulting from the application of the ISBDs will not normally be used by itself, but will form part of a complete entry in a catalogue or other bibliographic list. Organizational factors (headings, uniform titles, etc), filing devices and tracings, and

subject information, used within or for the arrangement of entries in a catalogue or other listing, do not form part of the ISBDs.

The ISBDs discussed in this book are:

1 *General international standard bibliographic description.* 1977 [ISBD (G)]
2 *International standard bibliographic description for non-book materials.* 1977 [ISBD(NBM)]
3 *International standard bibliographic description for printed music* (draft). To be publish 1979 [ISBD (PM)]

The sooner these become accepted throughout the world as the bases on which national codes for description are constructed the easier the interchange of information between libraries will be. This is particularly important for the international language of music.

CHAPTER ONE

PROBLEMS IN CATALOGUING MUSIC

THE PROBLEMS which have to be mastered in cataloguing a music library or in producing a printed catalogue or bibliography of music will obviously vary according to the kind of material being organized and the nature of the cataloguing process under consideration. The problems of cataloguing music literature are broadly the same as those to be solved in dealing with the subject literature in any other discipline. However, both music scores and recordings of music present problems of a special nature.

Further, in arriving at an author/composer heading for a catalogue entry, authors' or composers' names will present similar problems in music to those met with in any other subject; with the proviso that foreign names are more likely to be encountered in music because it is not dependent on language for its understanding. In fact it is reasonable to say that the majority of composers are not nationals of those countries which are part of the English speaking world. However, the matter of correct form of entry for names has received a lot of attention and satisfactory solutions are available for the vast majority of cases.

The success of the subject or form catalogue, for music as for other subjects, is directly affected by the quality of the classification scheme chosen to arrange items, either on the shelves or in the classified section of a catalogue or bibliography. This is because it is easier to produce a good index when a modern faceted scheme, such as BCM, rather than a traditional enumerative scheme, such as DC, is used as the foundation of the process. This will be demonstrated in the chapter on subject cataloguing.

Since the publication of the first edition of this book in 1966, there has been a considerable development in international co-operation in cataloguing with the publication of further volumes in the cataloguing code prepared by the IAML, two editions of AACR (1967 and 1978) and a series of ISBDs by IFLA. Of the latter, most importantly for music librarians, the ISBD (PM) will be published in 1979. In addition, with the development of the use of computers for the production of catalogues, the facility for the interchange of information in machine readable form between libraries, particularly the national libraries of the English speaking world, has increased enormously. Unfortunately, while the cataloguing of music literature has benefited by the latter development, music scores and sound recordings have remained relatively untouched and much remains to be done. This is particularly true of the United Kingdom, where there is still no national listing of sound recordings and the BCM is unsatisfactory as a national bibliography as its coverage remains far from comprehensive.

There are also more music libraries now than in 1966, particularly as, during the thriving years of the late 1960s and early 1970s, more and more local authorities in the United Kingdom established recorded sound libraries and linked them with their music collections. This process often benefited the latter, as in many areas the music stock was often increased in an attempt to give it parity with the record collection. In addition, many more colleges and polytechnics offer courses on music, and this has meant an increase in the number of music libraries in educational institutions. Partly because of the failure to date of the British Library to develop its cataloguing services for music and sound recordings, many of these libraries, both public and academic, remain relatively untouched by the busy international scene as far as their cataloguing of music is concerned. This accounts both for the success of the co-operative effort known now as BLCMP, which a number of music libraries have joined, and for the wide variations in practice found in music libraries throughout the country.

Some of the errors in catalogues could easily be avoided if librarians and cataloguers generally acknowledged that music librarians are not creating problems unnecessarily, and that it is advisable to have a knowledge of music when creating a catalogue of a music collection. It is a sad fact that there are libraries where for 'reasons of economy' music is catalogued centrally by cataloguers who lack a knowledge of the subject. The music librarian has subsequently to cope with the errors which speedily manifest themselves as the result of such false economy. It is possibly more important to have a knowledge of the subject in order to catalogue music successfully than it is to have the same background to be a music librarian. With the number of music graduates now entering the profession, there is less excuse than there was a few years ago for incompetence in the appointment of staff and the assignment of duties. It is hoped that the following survey of some typical problems met in cataloguing music will at least make librarians aware of some of the difficulties to be encountered and of the need for specific subject knowledge when cataloguing music.

Title page

A fundamental rule in all author cataloguing has been to use the title page as the primary source of information about any particular book. This has been maintained by the ISBD (G) and ISBD (M) and will be re-affirmed by the ISBD (PM) when it is published. Nevertheless, the latter does take full account of the problems which arise when this rule is applied to music. Some typical situations are:

1 *Title page missing*

A very common practice with music publishers is to supply a work with a paper cover and without a title page. The information normally supplied on the title page is given either on the cover or on the first page of the score. This practice is followed by all types of firms. For example, in 1937 the Oxford University Press published a piano arrangement of Walton's *Crown imperial* for which there is no title page. Copyright details are given on the first page of the score, but there is no indication that it is a piano arrangement, except on the cover. In neither place is there information about an arranger.

Furthermore, scores quite often receive rough physical treatment. This can mean that second-hand music which a library acquires may have lost its cover. In handling a score, such as the example by Walton quoted above, when it has lost its cover, the cataloguer without knowledge of music would be in some extra difficulty, for there would be no indication of the true nature of the work *ie* that it is an arrangement. The only advice that can be given is to be suspicious of all scores, and to have adequate bibliographical resources available for checking.

In cataloguing items to be included in a national bibliography or in any other catalogue likely to be used by scholars, it is proper to indicate the inclusion of information from sources other than the title page by enclosing such items in square brackets [ ], and to indicate the omission of information supplied on the title page by the use of the omission sign . . . , in order that a person using the bibliography or catalogue may have a precise picture of the nature of a publication. However, in other situations it may be simpler and more helpful to the reader to decide on an order in which the different parts of a catalogue entry are to be arranged, and to supply the necessary information for each part from any appropriate source. Readers will surely trust librarians to do their work honestly and will not be concerned with the source of the information provided. It would seem helpful in such circumstances to use the order of items prescribed by the appropriate ISBD as a basis for the layout of entries in this kind of catalogue, in order that as much uniformity in library practice as possible may be achieved. It must be quite clearly understood that there is no attempt to suggest here that one kind of reader is superior to another or, for example, that a scholar is more important than a performer. It is merely that their needs are different. The scholar may wish to examine many editions of a work and will need precise details about a library's holdings. The performer will normally be much more interested in the nature of the score and the kind of instruments and/or voices needed for realization of the work, and will not be particularly interested in the source of the information provided.

2 *Title pages in a foreign language*

Almost inevitably every library, however small, will receive among its music acquisitions some works with title pages in foreign languages. The music will be the same whatever the language, with directions for tempo, dynamics etc probably in Italian. This situation arises from the international nature of music publishing, in which a publisher may issue the same score in several countries at the same time, the only variation being that the title page will perhaps be printed in the language appropriate to each country. Many publishers do not even bother to do this, but sell the same edition with the same title page wherever it is required. Even when they have used title pages in different languages, publishers quite frequently sell these copies with little or no regard to the native language of the purchasing country, especially when an issue in one language has sold out. Thus the librarian who orders a particular title may receive the correct copy, but with the title page in a foreign language. For example, this work was found on the shelves of a small public library:

Collection Litoff/Sonates/pour/piano et violon/DE/ W A Mozart/ Nouvelle Edition/soigneusement revue par/JNN Rauch/Braunschweig/Henry Litoff's Verlag/.

The work is that of a German editor and publisher with a French title page in an English library! The mistake here would surely be to follow the title page without any modification. This would only result in the work being filed in the wrong place as far as users of the catalogue in the English speaking world are concerned. The solution here is to use a uniform title for all editions of a work. This method is fully explained later (see chapter 2).

Title pages in alphabets other than roman raise the problem of transliteration. This is a relatively easy matter when it is a question of dealing with non-roman title pages or those with names transliterated into English forms. A decision can be made to follow either the ALA/LC romanization tables or the British Standard (BS 2979 for Cyrillic and Greek characters) or the forms used in *Grove's dictionary of music and musicians*. The latter does have the distinct advantage for music libraries in that it is very widely used by musicians and therefore the form of name or title of a work used in it is probably familiar to them. However, the pressure of uniform practice suggests use of the ALA/LC tables. Tchaikovsky poses the main problem here, partly because of his popularity. He can appear under a variety of forms according to the system used, eg Chaikovskiĭ, Tschaikovsky.

It is interesting to note that AACR 2 has alternative rules for this problem. The rule in the text (22.3C2) requires romanization according to the table for the language adopted by the cataloguing agency. The alternative rule allows use of a form which has become well established in English-language reference sources. The national libraries have indicated their intention to use the alternative rule. The definition of 'well established' would appear to be the problem here.

However, there remains a further difficulty for the cataloguer of music. Mention has already been made of the likelihood of receipt of many editions with title pages in foreign languages, even for the standard repertoire. This means that transliteration into languages other than English may be quite common, with resulting strange forms such as Chatschaturjan for Khachaturian.

Another minor matter is the variation in the symbols or names used for the different keys in the major European languages. The English 'E flat major' is represented in German by 'Es-dur', and in France and Italy by 'mi bémol majeur'. Musicians do not generally need to remember these differences, as they rely on the key signature to indicate the key of a piece. Therefore, if the cataloguer copies the title page it is not much help to musicians, as foreign expressions for keys will not be familiar. The foreign terms must therefore be translated into English if the catalogue is to inform.

Sometimes the title page may have the title in more than one language. International usage as expressed in the ISBDs, AACR 2 and the IAML codes requires the transcribing of all the titles. For example the ISBD (G) gives the following result:

Le nozze di Figaro = Die Hochzeit des Figaro = The marriage of Figaro.

The sign = is the prescribed linking device for parallel titles. The ISBD (PM) will certainly have the same rule. Some libraries may well prefer to give just the English title or the original title rather than all three.

3 *Title page listing several works*

Music publishers frequently issue scores with title pages listing several works, the title relevant to the particular score sometimes being underlined. This kind of title page is frequently referred to as a passe-partout. For example there is an Augener edition of Schumann's *Etudes symphoniques*, opus 13, which lists on what is supposedly the title page all the piano works by that composer without any indication of the actual work contained therein. Presumably this is done so that the page can be easily used as an advertisement in other publications. Once again there is no point in following the title page literally. The title for the work included must be catalogued, with a note, if deemed necessary, on the nature of the title page.

4 *Title page order varies*

There is no agreed way of referring to music. This means that some title pages for a given work will have the form 'concerto for violin', others 'violin concerto'. Which of the two a library selects must depend on the approach its readers generally make, but it would be unhelpful always to follow the title page as this could result in separation of several editions of the same work, since entries for it would be filed in the sequence according to the different initial letters:

Concerto for piano no 5

Emperor concerto

Piano concerto no 5

Once again the practice of using a uniform title offers the best solution.

5 *Arrangements*

A situation in which the title page is often misleading is the very common case when an arrangement of the original piece has been made, either by simplifying it or by editing it for another instrument. The following is a particularly interesting example, where the title page reads:

To Sidney and Frances Colvin/Concerto/for/violoncello and orchestra/composed by/Edward Elgar/op 85/Arrangement for violoncello and piano/by the composer/

This provides unusually complete information, or so it seems until the contents of the work are examined, to reveal that it is a second arrangement of this work for viola and piano by Lionel Tertis. It is only the viola part which supplies this information, for the piano part is scored for piano with the cello line shown. Uniform titles are again helpful.

6 *Title page omits essential information*

Some of the earlier examples serve to underline the lack of essential information on music title pages, but there are many situations where the items omitted are so important that it is difficult to understand why they are not included. This is particularly true when a transposing instrument such as the clarinet is involved. For example, music for the A clarinet is scored for C major when the composer wishes it to sound in A major, while that for its close relative the B flat clarinet is scored for C major when the piece is in B flat major. The reasons for this are historical and complicated, but many players only possess a B flat instrument. It is vital, therefore, for the player to know for which instrument the music is arranged. Not all clarinettists can transpose as they play and the key in this case is really fundamental information about the score. Thus the following title page is incomplete:

Schumann/Fantasiestücke/für Klavier and Klarinette/oder Violine/ opus 73.

It does not say whether this is the arrangement for violin or clarinet, nor in the latter case does it say which instrument is required. In fact the piece was originally written for the A clarinet, but this particular score is for the B flat instrument. This can be confusing and does require care in cataloguing, as reliance on the title page can result in incomplete information.

It seems unfortunate that AACR 2 in its rules for uniform titles does not allow for indication of the key in which an instrument is pitched in the uniform title (rule 25.29D3):

clarinet *not* clarinet in A

saxophone *not* alto saxophone

Admittedly this information can be given in a note, but notes are not always read and such information does have significance for many players.

7 *Title page without useful identifying elements*

Frequently in identifying a piece of music three items are of great importance: opus number, number within a series and thematic catalogue number.

Opus 76 no 1

Symphony no 9 The new world

Sonata in B flat, D 960

In the case of the thematic catalogue number D 960, the letter stands for the initial letter of the surname of the compiler of the catalogue, Otto Erich Deutsch. This is the usual practice for thematic catalogue references:

K 622 Köchel/Mozart : clarinet concerto

H I 104 Hoboken/Haydn : symphony 104

The most celebrated exception is the use of BWV (Bach Werke Verzeichnis = Bach works catalogue) for Bach's compositions instead of S for Schmieder, the compiler, who felt it irreverent to associate his name with that of the great composer. Some libraries and bibliographies perfer to use S, however, for consistency.

Köchel's arrangement is chronological, therefore K 622 is a late work. Hoboken's arrangement is by form, then chronological. Thus group I is *symphonies*.

One of the safest methods of checking the details of a particular work is to use the thematic catalogue of the composer's works, if one has been issued. Once the work has been identified, the thematic catalogue number can be used in the catalogue entry even if the publisher has not supplied it. However, even thematic catalogues are not infallible. Thus Köchel's catalogue of Mozart's works, undoubtedly the most famous, has undergone changes in the numbering of works since the first edition (1862). As has been said, it arranges the works in chronological order. However, much has been learned about the history of Mozart's music over the last hundred years. In order to accommodate this new knowledge and some 'lost' works which have been rediscovered, as well as to remove some works now known not to be by Mozart, there have had to be changes in the numbering in recent editions. Fortunately this does not affect the majority of works, but care is needed in using the catalogue Even the comparatively recently published Hoboken catalogue of Haydn's works (Instrumental works 1957; Vocal works 1971; Indexes, addenda and corrigenda 1978) has been proved erroneous in a number of cases. For example, the Christa Landon edition of the piano sonatas (Vienna: Universal Edition, 1966. 4 v) provides a much more chronologically accurate numbering, and her system has been adopted in some catalogues using L or CL as the identifying symbol. There is no satisfactory thematic catalogue for Handel, but rumour has it that two are in preparation. This is only likely to cause further confusion to judge by the chaotic situation with Vivaldi and Scarlatti, for whom five and two thematic lists respectively are published. It is astonishing that with both the Longo and Kirkpatrick thematic lists available, record companies still issue recordings of Scarlatti's sonatas giving only the key. In such cases musical knowledge is essential if the works recorded are to be identified.

Failing a thematic catalogue, a collected edition of the composer's works can often by useful as a means of identification. Thus, in the case of Soler, his keyboard sonatas can be identified by using the numbering from the collected edition edited by Samuel Rubio (Madrid: Union musical española, 1962. 6 v). For Handel the nineteenth century Handelgesellschaft collected edition must be used, as unfortunately the modern edition is not completed yet. The method of identification is exactly the same as for a thematic catalogue, using R for Rubio in the case of Soler and HG from Handelgesellschaft for Handel. For a list of thematic catalogues reference should be made to the bibliography by Barry Brook (Brook 1972); for collected editions the work by Heyer (Heyer 1969) can be used. Finally, citations in standard reference works can help with identification.

Opus numbers are very useful, but composers do not use them consistently. Bartók reached opus 20 and then appears to have tired of this system. Even before then, according to the chronological list in the work on the composer by Halsey Stevens (2nd ed New York : OUP, 1964), Bartók omitted many works and opus 20 should have been numbered opus 57. Bartók was usually a very systematic composer, so it is no matter for surprise that other, less orderly, composers' opus numbers are even more confused and that they are used inconsistently by publishers. Nevertheless, if they exist but are not given on the title page, they should be supplied in the catalogue entry.

Numbers of works in series (*eg* symphonies, quartets) are extremely useful, but are sometimes not supplied by publishers, or else are incorrectly given. Perhaps the best known example of the confusion which can occur here is in the symphonies of Dvořak, totalling nine but until recently in this country generally thought to be only five. The inclusion of the four earlier symphonies in the canon has meant renumbering the later five. Consequently, many libraries must have scores or recordings of two number fives. Publishers and record companies still sometimes ignore these developments, so that care is needed to ensure correct numbering. Another common trap is Schubert's *symphony no 9*, more correctly identified as no 7. Many references to the earliest quartet by Haydn refer to it as 'no 0' as it did not appear in the original list, Haydn himself having classified it as a divertimento. Anthony van Hoboken in his thematic catalogue of Haydn's works has kept it as a divertimento. The Hoboken thematic catalogue number is now the safest identification, even if the designation 'string quartet' is used: string quartet, H II 6. The designation 'Op 1, no 0' can be inserted as a further means of identification. Sometimes publishers refer to this work as 'Op 1, no 1', but this should be used for another earlier work in B flat.

This matter has been discussed at some length because some cataloguers assume too readily that it is easy to identify music by means of opus and series numbers.

8 *Imaginative titles*

These are often essential as a means of identification, especially when handling categories such as operas or songs. However, there are two occasions when their use raises problems.

The first is the choice between original and translated title, as quite often a work will be equally well known by both. It is difficult to frame a satisfactory rule which results in consistent application by cataloguers. Compare *The magic flute, La clemenza di Tito, The merry wives of Windsor, Cosi fan tutte* and *The nutcracker* or *casse-noisette*. No one has been able to find a common pattern to these which might offer the basis for a solution acceptable in all libraries.

The second problem arises from the frequency with which a distinctive title is added to a work not normally bearing one by persons other than the composer. Thus Berlioz's *Symphonie fantastique* (or *Fantastic symphony*) can be quite safely identified by this title, as it was so named by the composer. Haydn's *Mass* no 9 in D minor, on the other hand, has various additional titles in different countries: *Nelson, Imperial, Coronation*. In England it is now quite commonly referred to as *The Nelson mass*, although earlier it was called *The Imperial mass*. The autograph manuscript has 'missa' as its title, but Haydn entered it in his own catalogue as *Missa in Angustiis* (Mass in time of fear) and this is now becoming more accepted in England. To avoid confusion the distinctive title should not be used here. Entry under *Mass no 9, D minor* is to be preferred. Distinctive titles can be added at the end if necessary, however great the temptation may be to prefer entry under *Moonlight sonata, New world symphony* etc. References must of course be made from these popular names to the chosen heading.

9 *Duplication of one title*

A further special problem with music, which may result in related items being scattered throughout the entries under a composer if care is not taken, is the amount of duplication in relation to a title which may occur because of the different forms in which that work may appear. To take an extreme example of an opera, a library will have to consider acquiring the following: full score, vocal score, orchestral parts, arrangements of various melodies from the opera for individual voices and instruments, the libretto, the disc of the opera, the cassette of the opera, recordings of individual arias, and literature about the opera. Within each category there may be hundreds of items from which to choose. This does not seem to occur to the same extent with most other subjects.

The problems discussed so far arise almost entirely from the methods used by music publishers. It has long seemed to music librarians that their lives would be a good deal easier if some form of standardization was brought into music publishing, particularly regarding the identification of works on their title pages. The British Standards Institution has published a number of bibliographical standards in recent years, and one of these (BS 4754, 1971) relates to *Presentation of bibliographical information in printed music*. Like many standards, this has so far had very little impact, but a committee to revive the standard was set up in 1977 and the participation of music publishers has been greater this time. Also representatives of professional musicians have become involved and the terms of reference have been widened to take in printing and the physical presentation of the score. The draft standard *Recommendations for the presentation of music scores and parts* has been produced and sent to many organizations for comments. Even when the revised standard is printed acceptance will be slow, but improved standards of publication must surely come and can only help the cataloguer.

Recordings

Most of the above difficulties apply equally to recordings of music, apart from those which are obviously unique to music publishing such as the passepartout title page. A problem which is special to recordings is the difficulty of deciding in many cases who has primary responsibility for the items recorded on the disc or cassette under consideration and therefore under whom the main entry should be made. This would seem to be reasonably clear for classical recordings of a single work. The composer is the author and most searches for Mahler's *fifth symphony* will begin at *Mahler*. However, there have been suggestions made in some quarters in recent years that the conductor's name will often be the primary sought term in such cases and that the main entry would be more suitably placed under *Barbirolli* or *Karajan* as appropriate. This suggestion, which cannot be seriously sustained, arises probably from the desire to achieve consistency for all styles of music in the face of increased provision in libraries of styles other than classical and from the fact there is a much greater claim for entry under the performer(s) when recordings of jazz, rock, folk etc are being catalogued. There is also a more significant claim to be made for the performer in examples such as *Janet Baker sings English songs*. These would seem in reality to be examples of a fairly straightforward situation, where different kinds of recordings require radically different treatment.

In the case of recordings of styles such as jazz, rock and those in the popular field, it is also often difficult to establish who is the composer. Each item on a recording has listed by it a string of names with no assignment of responsibilities between author of text, composer and arranger. It is often suggested that the last name is the composer's. (Thus AACR 1 Rule 250A : an arbitary choice for main entry must be made, the *final* name listed being chosen as most probably that of the composer). Here are the credits from four different recordings of *Progy and Bess*, where there is no doubt as to the composer:

George Gershwin, Ira Gershwin and Dubose Heyward
Gershwin–Heyward–Gershwin
George Gershwin–Dubose Heyward–Ira Gershwin
G & I Gershwin–Heyward

These totally contradict the statement in AACR 1. It is not suggested that AACR 1 was wrong. It merely reflects the confusion in the record industry! More often than not the names are those of those persons totally unknown to the cataloguer.

G Fragos/J Baker/D Gasparre

are the names against a number on a Duke Ellington disc. It is obvious here that entry must be under *Ellington*, as it must be under *Baker* for the Janet Baker recording given above. But there are many recordings which present problems if the principle of main entry is still followed, eg *Songs of Bob Dylan sung by Joan Baez*. AACR2 (rule 21.23B) requires entry under *Dylan* with added entry under *Baez*. In this style of music the issue is not as clear as such a rule suggests.

Dylan and Baez are probably of equal status, but there are many situations when the performer is more famous than the composer eg *Change of scenes* with music by Francy Boland and with Stan Getz as principal performer. It is likely that *Getz* will be the more sought term here. Perhaps this is a very strong argument for the use of the principle of multiple entry rather than the traditional one of main entry.

Libraries which cannot afford the luxury of a large number of entries for each item in their catalogues really face quite a sharp problem here, as the number of entries for an item can be quite high. This is especially true when the item under consideration is a boxed set of (say) three discs, each of them having sixteen bands. This makes a total of fourty eight items to be catalogued, each having perhaps a composer and several named performers. To catalogue under both composers and performers for each work in the set will result in a minimum total of 96 entries for the album. In terms of time and cost that is a daunting and, for the cataloguer, probably a tedious prospect. A national collection will have to make these entries, but other librarians may justifiably feel that some simpler solution must be found. But if only entries for the boxed set as a complete unit are made, then the problem of choice of entry terms becomes more acute.

Ethnomusicology

The rapidly developing interest in ethnomusicology is revealed by the number of British institutions offering courses–fifteen in 1978 as against none in 1958. Harold Samuel in a recent article (Samuel 1977) claims that ethnomusicology is growing faster than any other discipline. The main source of information is undoubtedly recorded material. Composer and performer are scarcely significant in this area, and main entry is generally required under a geographical entity, eg a region or an ethnic group. At the British Institute of Recorded Sound it is intended to make the geographical factor the primary arranging element for entries in the catalogue. There is general dissatisfaction in the United States with the LC subject headings list as far as its treatment of non-western music is concerned. This has led the Music Library Association to establish a Sub-committee on Music other than western-art. The impression gained is that LC subject headings scatter culturally related areas (Kaufmann 1977. p 1). There is a tendency for some librarians to be defensive on this issue and say that ethnomusicology can be accommodated within current practice. But the fact remains that all the present methods are heavily biased towards western thought and that ethnomusicologists are very unhappy with the coverage national bibliographies and library catalogues give to their subject. Thus the treatment of ethnomusicological recordings and other documents poses an urgent problem.

Non-musical materials

Another difficulty which music librarians face is that as a part of their duties they are often expected to handle all kinds of recorded sound. It is obviously beyond the scope of this book to discuss the cataloguing of recordings on childbirth without fear, birdsong, the second world war and railway engines, but such items can form quite a sizeable part of the record collection and can occupy a great deal of time. Until all libraries arrange all materials on an individual subject together, so that recordings of Shakespeare's plays are placed with the texts rather than with the symphonies of Beethoven, music librarians will have to spend their time on what, for their main purpose, is a pointless task, however much they may enjoy the plays. Adequate cataloguing of these non-musical items can take much effort.

Conclusion

The purpose of this survey of problems is not to be exhaustive nor to prove how difficult the music cataloguers's task can be. It is intended to demonstrate the existence of problems of which the non-musician may not always be aware, and to try to show how a few of the more central ones might be solved. Experienced cataloguers without musical knowledge can cope with these problems provided they accept that they exist and seek appropriate guidance for their solution. Nevertheless, life is made easier by using the experience and knowledge which a cataloguer with a knowledge of music has. The service to readers will be much more effective.

The rest of this book is concerned with an examination of the treatment which various published codes and libraries accord these and other problems.

CHAPTER TWO

UNIFORM TITLES

UNIFORM TITLES have now become widely accepted as a means of coping with the problems raised by the lack of information on music title pages. This acceptance largely arose from their extensive use in AACR 1 to solve problems not only for music but also for sacred books, anonymous works without titles, peace treaties and laws. For some of these categories uniform titles have been used for a long time. For music, however, their adoption appears to have been somewhat slower, although some libraries particularly in the United States, have used them for much longer. Rules for their application first appeared in the US in 1941 in the *Code for cataloging music* issued by the Music Library Association, with uniform titles defined as conventional titles.

Definitions and basic practices

They are defined in AACR 2 as:

1 The particular title by which a work that has appeared under varying titles is to be identified for cataloguing purposes.
2 A conventional collective title used to collocate publications of an author, composer or corporate body containing several works or extracts etc from several works, eg complete works, several works in a particular literary or musical form.

The purpose of uniform titles is to provide a more logical order of entries in a catalogue by devizing a title which will serve to bring together in the catalogue entries for all editions, translations, arrangements etc of a single work, whatever appears on the title page. They also collocate under the same title all subject entries relating to the work and any added entries for works related to it.

The usual practice is to place the uniform title on a separate line between the heading selected for the entry and the transcription of the title proper. Thus to catalogue the following work without using a uniform title would result in the entry shown:

Wilhelm Hansen Edition No 959 B/The Four temperaments/Die vier Temperamente/for orchestra/Carl Nielsen op 16/Miniature score

Nielsen, Carl
The four temperaments = Die vier Temperamente op. 16 . . .

A further title (*Symphonie No 2*) appears at the head of the first page of the score. This provides the uniform title which unfortunately cannot always be obtained so easily. Adding the uniform title, the entry now takes the form:

Nielsen, Carl
[Symphonies, no. 2, op 16]
The four temperaments = Die vier Temperamente op 16 . . .

It is inappropriate to add the key to the uniform title for Nielsen's symphonies, but in the case of pre-twentieth century works AACR 2 requires it to be added (rule 25.31A5):

Franck, César
[Quintet, piano, strings, F minor]
Quintet F minor for pianoforte, 2 violins, viola and violoncello . . .

In the case of twentieth century works the key should be stated if it is given prominently in the work.

If the composer only wrote one work in a particular form or genre, the singular noun for the form or genre is used, as in the Franck example; otherwise the plural is used, as for Nielsen's symphony (rule 25.27B). The form *quintet, piano, strings* is one of several allowed by rule 25.29C for standard chamber music combinations.

A basic uniform title, following AACR 2 usage, for a composer for whom there is as yet no recognized thematic catalogue takes the form:

Mendelssohn Bartholdy, Felix
[Symphonies, no 4, op. 90, a major]
Symphony 4 A major "Italian" op. 90

Square brackets are used in AACR 2 as shown in these examples, but they are not essential and their omission is permitted by the code.

The IAML *Rules for full cataloging* (IAML 3) uses the term 'filing titles' rather than 'uniform titles' and defines it (2.1) as:

A title added in an entry in order to bring together in the catalog all editions and arrangements of a work. For works of personal or corporate authorship the filing title is placed immediately below the heading, enclosed in square brackets. For works of unknown authorship, the filing title heading is placed on the line above the title transcription. A filing title is used when a work is published with title in a language other than that of the first edition, or varying from that of the first edition; when a composer has written more than one work having the same title; or when the publication consists of an excerpt from a larger work.

A footnote defines the use of the word 'work' here as:

A complete musical composition, whether it is conceived as a single independent composition, or as a set consisting of several pieces, normally with a single opus number.

Excerpts are parts of a work.

These rules appear to aim at a somewhat shorter uniform title than that required by AACR 2. Thus an entry for

Concerto no 4/G major/for Pianoforte and orchestra/by/Ludwig van Beethoven/op 58

using AACR 2 (rules 25.31A1-A5) gives

[Concertos, piano, no. 4 op 58, G major]

while using IAML 3 (rules 2.412 and 2.43) gives

[Concertos. Piano. Op 58]

Notice further the different punctuation.

Neither code appears to favour the addition of popular epithets in the uniform or filing title, such as required by AACR 1 (British text) rule 235:

[Sonata, piano, no 14, op 27, no.2, C sharp minor, (Moonlight)]

Rule 26.4A1 in AACR 2 ('See' references for uniform titles) has an example which quite clearly indicates that they are not to be used:

Beethoven, Ludwig van
    Moonlight sonata
        see Beethoven Ludwig van
            Sonatas, piano, no. 14, op 27, no 2, C♯ minor

AACR 2 (rule 25.31A6) does allow as a last resort the use of any other identifying element if the numeric identifying elements, key, year of composition or year of original publication are not sufficient or available, to distinguish one work from another. IAML 3 does not apparently allow them to be used under any circumstances and indeed the example under rule 2.43 specifically omits the ephithet from the filing title:

Prokof'ev, Sergei Sergeevich
[Symphonies. Op. 25]
Classical symphony

The lack of indentation here follows the layout in IAML 3. The earlier examples above accord with that in AACR 2.

Use of thematic catalogues

When a thematic catalogue to a composer's works is available, its numbering system is preferred by both codes before serial or opus numbers. Thus AACR 2 (example for rule 25.33) and IAML 3 (example for rule 2.412) specify the use of numbers from Deutsch's thematic index to Schubert's compositions in preference to serial numbers. This is sensible, as the use of thematic index numbers clearly identifies the work under scrutiny. Popular libraries might still wish to use the serial number in the case of some composers, preferring

Symphonies, no 6, D589
to Symphonies, D589

But standards of accuracy must continue to be raised and the use of thematic indexes when they are recognized as authoritative, as in the case of Deutsch, needs to be encouraged. D944 is much better than no 9 in the case of Schubert's *Symphony no 9(7)*, as there is doubt about the serial number here, as there is in many other cases. K numbers have now become well recognized by the general public for many of Mozart's works. To use thematic index numbers in this way implies alteration of existing entries, of course, when an authoritative index to a composer's works appears for the first time. It is a pity that neither code picks up the practice of using collected edition numbers when no recognized thematic index exists, but that is no reason for not using such devices as long as the symbol is clearly explained to users of the catalogue.

Distinctive titles

Both codes require the use of the original form in the case of imaginative or distinctive titles, though the suggested basis is somewhat different. AACR 2's rule 25.27A requires the use of the composer's original title in the language in which it was formulated. This gives:

Rimskiĭ-Korsakov, N.A.
[Zolotoĭ petushok. . .]
The golden cockerel. . .

IAML 3 (2.421) states: 'Use the title of the first edition, in modern orthography. . .' This gives the same result as AACR 2 for *The golden cockerel*, but both rules have a secondary statement:

If, however, a later title in the same language is better known, use it (AACR 2)

. . .Unless the work has come to be better known by a later title (IAML 3).

Would the latter allow *Le coq d'or* or *The golden cockerel* in perference to the Russian title? AACR 2 is firmer and therefore somewhat simpler to follow consistently, although it will not be easy for all libraries to establish the title used in the first edition. Many libraries in fact may prefer the alternative footnote rule in IAML 3:

When the title of the first edition is in a language not commonly read by the clientele of a particular library, translate the title into the language of the cataloguing library, unless there is a well known translation, in which case it should be used.

That definitely allows *The golden cockerel* to be used. Of course references must be made whatever title is used as the uniform title, from all other forms not used, both in their own right as titles and from entry under the composer:

Bartók, Béla
[A Kékszakállú herceg vára]
Bluebeard's castle = Herzog Blaubart's Burg

with references from:

Bluebeard's castle
Herzog Blaubart's Burg
Le château de Barbe-Bleue

and from each of these titles under the composer's name, eg

Bluebeard's castle (Bartók)
see Bartók, Béla
A Kékszakállú herceg vára

Bartók, Béla
Bluebeard's castle
see Bartók, Béla
A Kékszakállú herceg vára

This is an interesting example, as the first edition was issued with Hungarian, German, French and English texts. With knowledge of Bartók's fierce patriotism, there is no doubt about which is the basic text. Nationals of countries outside Hungary might find entry under the Hungarian form rather daunting. This is true of most of Bartók's titles in their first editions. Does AACR 2 really require entry under the Hungarian, when even the Hungarians recognize the difficulty of their language and publish texts on Bartók simultaneously in the main

European languages? The situation is further complicated here by the fact that the opera sometimes has the English title *Duke Bluebeard's castle* and that other composers have written operas with very similar titles:

Grétry : Raoul Barbe-Bleue
Offenbach : Barbe-Bleue
Dukas : Ariane et Barbe-Bleue
Razniček : Ritter Blaubart

Some of these have familiar English titles. Offenbach's *Bluebeard* has been performed in the same season as Bartók's version. Confusion is bound to arise between titles.

This work underlines the difficulty here. There is much to be said for the consistency which results from use of the title found in the first edition. The value of consistency in catalogues cannot be too strongly emphasized. Added entries and references alleviate the problem of search patterns which start at alternative titles, but it is irritating to be referred frequently to another point in the catalogue. Multiple entry is ultimately the only solution, but that can be very costly. Whenever possible, the basic rules of both codes should be followed, but if a library feels that the majority of its users are going to prefer titles in their own language, then the footnote alternatives in IAML 3, to which reference has already been made, should be preferred.

Generic titles

So far the use of uniform titles has only been discussed in very general terms with specific examples used to illustrate the application of what could be termed the basic rules which provide help in dealing with both imaginative titles and those titles which constitute a very large part of the classical repertoire such as *sonata, symphony* and *concerto*. These are generally referred to as generic titles, their function being to indicate a musical form or genre. There is some disagreement between AACR 2 and IAML 3 on what types of musical compositions can be defined as forms or genres. Thus AACR 2 in a footnote to rule 25.27B states:

> The name of a type of composition, as distinguished from a distinctive title, is considered to be the name of a form (concerto, symphony, trio-sonata), a genre (capriccio, nocturne, intermezzo), or a generic term frequently used by different composers (movement, muziek, Stück). Other titles are generally considered to be distinctive (chamber concerto, Konzertstück, little piano suite, Übung).

IAML 3 in a note (2.41) states:

> The number of titles which are also the names of musical forms (eg Fugue) or genre (eg Quartet) are limited. Such titles as Voluntary, Intermezzo, Ricercare, Lied etc do not fall into this category. Titles which do not consist solely of the names of musical forms are treated under 2.42 eg Kammersonate, Missa Brevis, Double Quartet, Sonata da chiesa, Scherzo fantastique, etc. In case of doubt, catalog according to 2.42.

The rule referred to here (2.42) deals with distinctive titles and has already been examined. It will be observed that IAML 3's definition does not accept the terms which are genres according to AACR 2 eg intermezzo. Unfortunately, it does not make its understanding of the word 'genre' very clear, quoting only *quartet* and *sextet*, the latter in an example. The problem of what constituties a genre is crucial because rule 2.3 in IAML 3 states:

> For those titles consisting solely of the name of a musical form or genre, all of the elements in the filing title are given in the language of the cataloguing library. For all other titles, elements other than the title proper are given in the language of the library

and rule 25.27B in AACR 2 has:

> If the title selected according to 25.27A [concerned with using composer's original title] consists solely of the name of one type of composition, use the accepted English form of name if there are cognate forms in English, French, German and Italian, or if the same name is used in all these languages...

The rules are giving the same instruction, but neither is very clear on what is meant by genre. Two books on music, among many, define form, indicating quite clearly that it is a problem to say what actually constitutes a form in musical terms:

> ...It would be impossible to find a definition [of form] which would be likely to meet with the universal approval of musicians and scholars... Many writers use the term in a wider sense, including in it, what might be more properly termed "stylistic types" eg the chaconne and the passacaglia (which are stylistic types of variation form), or the allemande, courante etc (which are stylistic types of binary form). Others prefer to use it in a narrower sense, by restricting its application to those schemes which are based on the principle of repetition [eg Variation form, Rondo, Rondeau]

Willi Apel in the *Harvard dictionary of music* (Heinemann, 1944)

This article distinguishes between these repetition forms, continuation forms (motets, choral compositions, ricercare, fugue etc) and compound forms consisting of various movements (sonata, concerto, suite, mass, cantata etc).

R O Morris in *The structure of music* OUP, 1935 p viii) approaches the problem of definition from a slightly different angle again, but comes to a similar conclusion:

> We have first of all to distinguish names that imply a certain type of structure or a certain grouping of movements–eg rondo, suite–from those which have merely a vague association with the style or content of the musical thought–eg rhapsody, impromptu, nocturne... it will be found that the number of genuine archetypes in music is not very large.

Both these quotations demonstrate that musical form is seen as being concerned with structure; genre is a term not very widely used among musicians in this context, but dictionaries define the word to mean kind and (in art) style. So there is very little help for cataloguers here. The problem is not really a musical one so much as a matter of definition and whether to use the cataloguer's own language or the foreign term. AACR 2's rule 25.27B concludes with the sentence:

> Do not use the English form of name for works intended for concert performance called *étude, fantasia,* or *sinfonia concertante* or their cognates.

Chopin's études? Chopin's studies? *The Shorter Oxford dictionary* gives *études* as acceptable English usage for a musical composition of its type, so a cataloguer using this form of the word would not appear to be using other than acceptable English. No one would surely want to use *fancy* or *fantasy* for *fantasia* or *concerted symphony* for *sinfonia concertante*. Surely the point for all these terms is that they are accepted as English usage. The real difficulty with étude/study is the decision about the purpose of composition. Chopin's études are probably the most famous and they were certainly intended as studies, of which they are quite outstanding examples as indeed they are of concert pieces. To follow this rule means having two sequences under each word when a choice of one of them would surely meet all cases. Étude, according to several dictionaries, has become the accepted word in most European languages including English, if not precisely in that form at least in something very easily identifiable as it. Étude should therefore be preferred in English. Finally, if a *sinfonia concertante* is not intended for concert performance, what is its purpose?

Trio sonatas

Both codes suggest the use of this term for the Baroque *sonata a tre*. The use of the word sonata at the beginning of the period around 1600 was purely to distinguish a piece intended to be played (suonare) from piece intended to be sung (cantare). Giovanni Gabrieli used the term extensively to designate pieces written for several instruments. He seems to have interchanged it with *canzona* in applying it to such compositions in the same form. The Baroque was a very exciting period musically and composers seem to have used terms fairly indiscriminately.

It is from their freedom of usage that some of our contemporary cataloguing confusions over terms such as *fantasia, prelude, chaconne* etc arise. The term sonata began gradually to be applied in a variety of ways:

1 Sonata da camera (chamber sonata): a series of dance movements.
2 Sonata da chiesa (church sonata): a series of movements which were not in dance form.
3 Sonata a tre or sonata a quattro: sonata for three or four melody instruments plus continuo of one or more instruments, making a total of at least four and five instruments respectively.

This last point causes confusion, as it seems very strange to apply the term *sonata a tre* (trio sonata) to a piece requiring four instruments, but it merely reflects the supporting role of the continuo. The so-called 'solo' sonata causes yet more confusion, as the continuo was usually performed by two instruments, making a total of three; in performance, therefore, a solo sonata looks more like a trio sonata than does a sonata in three parts! There is of course further difficulty in the cross classification between definitions 1 and 2 (forms of composition) on the one hand and 3 (number of instruments) on the other. However, all was resolved eventually when the term *sonata de camera* was replaced by *suite* for sets of dances and the term *sonata* came to be applied to other pieces without the *da chiesa*. To play or listen to Baroque music only adds to the confusion of definition as the two forms quite often sound very much alike. Some *da camera* movements would be very difficult as a dance and some *da chiesa* movements would be quite delightful for dancing. Some of Bach's most 'serious' music occurs in his suites of dances.

The purpose of this digression is to underline the confusion that existed in the Baroque about the use of the word *sonata*. In one sense, however, they were not confused. Almost without exception their titles begin 'Sonata. . .'. The *trio sonata* is a modern invention:

Corelli : Sonata da chiesa a tre
Zelenka : Sonata a due Hautbois et Basson con due bassi obligati
Bach : Sonatas (for two manuals and pedal BWV 525-530)
Purcell : Sonatas of III parts

The Zelenka example has a nice mixture of languages and is in fact a sonata a tre. The bassoon is also one of the due bassi obligati. But why for all these examples do the codes introduce the term *trio sonata*? Why not just *sonata*? The fact that it is a different form from the sonata of the classical period is of no significance. No one seems to worry about using the term *symphony* to apply to compositions which vary enormously in their structure. Is the resemblance between a symphony by Haydn and the new one by Peter Maxwell Davies any greater than that between a sonata by Purcell and one by Haydn? Yet it is perfectly acceptable in cataloguing them to use the term *symphony* for both of the former, but not *sonata* for the latter even though these are the terms used by the composers.

To conclude this discussion on forms and genres it seems reasonable to suggest that AACR 2 offers the best solution in practice provided the footnote to rule 25.27B is ignored and the concern is then with types of compositions. Further, as has been said above, terms such as *étude, fantasia* or *sinfonia concertante* can be treated as acceptable English forms. *Fancy* is acceptable, of course, for English works.

Designation of instruments

AACR 2 has many more rules on this part of the uniform title. IAML 3 is, however, very clear, requiring the addition of medium of performance when neither opus nor thematic index is available (rule 2.413) and there is one person to a part and no more than five parts:

Mozart, Wolfgang Amadeus
[Concertos, K 503]
Concerto for piano in C

Kozeluch, Leopold
[Concertos. Piano & orchestra. D major]
Piano concerto in D major

AACR 2 on the other hand works out a whole series of cases, while its basic approach is in a few respects similar to that in IAML 3. For example, fairly obviously, the cataloguer is not to add the medium of performance if it is implied by the title with such terms as Symphony (implied medium : orchestra), Mass (implied medium : voices, accompanied or not) etc. The medium *is* supplied, however, in such cases as Couperin's organ masses, which do not conform to the usual vocal medium (rule 25.29A2):

Couperin, François
[Masses, organ]
Messe, à L'usage des Paroisses. Messe propre pour les Convents

Further, if the medium is complex, some other statement such as thematic index or opus number is to be used.

Mozart, Wolfgang Amadeus
[Serenade, K 361]
Serenade for thirteen wind instruments. . .

However, there is a fundamental difference between the two codes on the actual filing of uniform titles. As shown in the examples above, IAML 3 requires priority to be given to the thematic index number whenever one is available. Failing that, an opus number is used if possible. AACR 2 on the other hand quite clearly requires medium of performance to come first. Examples from each code illustrate this:

IAML 3 rule 2.43

Milhaud, Darius
[Sonatas. Piano No 2]
Deuxième sonate pour piano

Mozart, Wolfgang Amadeus
[Sonatas. K 300]
Piano sonata in A major

AACR 2 rule 25.32B1

Schubert, Franz
[Impromptus, piano, D.899]

This means that in catalogues using IAML 3 the filing medium, whenever practicable, is the thematic index or opus number, whereas in catalogues using AACR 2 the filing medium is primarily medium of performance when it is appropriate to name one. Mozart wrote violin sonatas as well as piano sonatas. Using IAML 3 these will interfile with each other according to the Köchel number. IAML 3 is, however, an *international* code in the fullest sense of the word and the committee had to think of exchange of information between many different linguistic groups. Thus in the code itself the Milhaud example appears in the German text as follows:

Milhaud, Darius
[Sonaten. Klavier. Nr. 2]
Deuxième sonate pour piano

It is interesting here that, in a union catalogue of entries from different countries, further editing of the filing title would be required to bring all the entries for this work together, whereas entry under the title as it appears on the title page would not necessitate this. This applies, of course, only as long as there is only one publication of a work. As soon as an edition appears with (say) *Piano sonata no 2* as its title, the advantage of entry under the title from the title page disappears. The use of thematic index or opus numbers solves this problem on an international basis for a very large number of works.

AACR 2 is primarily a code to be used in the English speaking world, but it is based as far as possible on the *Paris principles* and the ISBDs with inter-language co-operation in mind. Perhaps more consideration should have been to this question of filing, especially when, as has already been shown (p 34), preference is given to the thematic index number over the series number in the case of symphonies. There is inconsistency in approach here at the very least. As Virginia Cunningham rightly points out in the introduction to IAML 3 (p 13), use of the medium produces an alphabetico-classed catalogue within an author sequence and attempts to satisfy a subject approach, which is not the function of an author catalogue. Even so IAML 3 does have an alternative rule allowing use of the medium (footnote to 2.412). Presumably this is for the benefit of smaller libraries unlikely to be involved in international exchange of catalogue information.

Number of performers

Care must be taken over the method of indicating how many performers there are. IAML 3 allows use of medium of performance only when there is one person to a part and no more than five parts. Unfortunately, it provides no information on how to indicate the presence of more than one part for the same instrument, but, if taken literally, the rule appears to mean that the entry for the sextet by Vincent d'Indy for two violins, two violas, two cellos (assuming for argument's sake that the opus number is missing) would be in the form:

[Sextet]

AACR 2 prefers entry under medium again:

[Sextet, violins, violas, cellos]

If the number of instruments is implied elsewhere in the uniform title the number of parts to each instrument is not stated.

The full statement of instruments for this non-standard chamber combination accords with rule 25.29C. Otherwise rule 25.29A3 states that only three elements are to be given in the order:

a) voices
b) keyboard instrument if there is more than one non-keyboard instrument
c) the order of other instruments in the score being catalogued

The examples in the code illustrate its general application clearly, but what they do not do is indicate how c) is applied when only parts are supplied by the publisher. This is a fairly common occurrence. Rule 25.29H1 indicates clearly how the limitation to three elements is achieved in certain cases by using such phrases as men's solo voices, women's solo voices. For compositions which include solo voices and chorus only, the appropriate terms for the chorus, drawn from 25.29H2, and accompaniment (if any) are to be given. Unfortunately, no example is given to show what is meant, but if it means what it says then this entry is correct:

Bach, Johann Sebastian
[Cantata, mixed voices, orchestra, continuo, BWV 159]
Cantata no 159 'Sehet wir gehn hinauf gen Jerusalem' for contralto, tenor, bass chorus and orchestra.

For comment on this form of entry for Bach's cantatas see below (p 44).

Rule 25.29C has a list of standard combinations which are frequently met in chamber music with their corresponding statement in the uniform title, eg for the string quartet the form used is

[Quartets, strings. . .]

This again differs from IAML 3 when thematic index or opus number is available:

Beethoven, Ludwig van
[Quartets, strings, op 18]

whereas IAML 3 would give:

[Quartets. Op 18]

For individual instruments both codes allow the English form of name to be used, AACR 2 even offering alternatives for English and American practice in some cases:

cor anglais *or* English horn.

For comment on the compulsory omission of pitch values under rule 25.29D3 in AACR 2 see page 23.

Voices

The general rules for statement of voices has already been covered by the basic rules in both codes on the statement of medium of performance as these apply equally to instruments and voices. IAML 3 is not very generous with examples of the treatment of vocal music:

Enumerate voices and instruments (in modern score order)

(Rule 2.413)

Unfortunately, almost all the examples are of instrumental music. Also the phrase 'in modern score order' is not very helpful. The order in modern scores is reasonably fixed for standard instruments, but there are many variations in order between scores from different publishing sources when it comes to less familiar instruments not used in the basic symphony orchestra. This is especially true of scores of modern music, when many unusual instruments are being used. The British Standard on presentation of music will hopefully improve the situation here.

One of the reasons why there are fewer examples of vocal music in IAML 3 is probably because most vocal music, following from its association with words, tends to have a distinctive title:

Die Winterreise

Aïda

St Matthew Passion

It also explains why the rules in AACR 2 for vocal music, where the title consists solely of a type of music, are straightforward for the most part. However, rule 25.29H1 has an example:

[Cantata, sopranos (2), alto, orchestra. . .]

This can only mean that Bach's cantatas must be entered in this way. Yet almost universal practice is to list them under BWV number. This is certainly the result IAML 3 gives:

[Cantatas. BWV 159]

This is how the example on p 43 would be entered following IAML 3. This is another example of AACR 2's unfortunate habit of constructing an alphabetico-classed catalogue in its uniform titles. If classification is needed for these cantatas, then surely it will be done on the shelves. The last place where it should be done is in the author catalogue.

The use of *canzoni* in the example under Maschera to illustrate rule 25.29J is probably influenced by the adoption of this form (canzone, canzoni) in the *Shorter Oxford dictionary*, but a number of music dictionaries and reference works use the form canzona(s). This is also the form given for English in the new polyglot dictionary of music (*Terminorum musicae index septem lingus redactus*. Kassel, Bärenreiter, 1978) Rule 25.27B states:

> . . . use the accepted English form of name if there are cognate forms in English, French, German and Italian, or if the same name is used in all these languages.

The polyglot dictionary must surely become the accepted guide to cognate terms in interpreting this rule. For *canzone* (Italian) it gives Kanzone (German), canzona (English), canzone or canzona (French).

Excerpts

For excerpts AACR 2 uses the word 'parts'. This is unfortunate in view of the special musical meaning of this word; it is also unnecessary as the word 'excerpt' used by IAML 3 can be substituted. Both codes recommend the same treatment of excerpts, which puts them under the heading for the main work:

Verdi, Giuseppe
[Rigoletto. Bella figlia dell'amor]

Bartók, Béla
[Mikrokosmos. No 121 Two-part study.]

Excerpts from a symphony etc are more clearly shown by indicating the number of the movement rather than its tempo as in the example in both codes from Beethoven's symphony no 1.

The treatment of more than one excerpt published together is similar in both codes, except that AACR 2 under rule 25.6B1 allows for the treatment of any sequence of consecutive and numbered excerpts from a work under the heading for the main work:

Bartók, Béla
[Mikrokosmos. Nos 1-21]

while IAML 3 seems to imply that the heading used would be:

Bartók, Béla
[Mikrokosmos. Selections]

If the excerpts are not numbered or not in sequence, then AACR 2 uses the same form as IAML 3-

Rossini, Gioacchino
[La cambiale di matrimonio. Selections]

Collected works

Both codes require the same uniform or filing title:

Schütz, Heinrich
[Works]

The real problem here is the choice of heading for a collection containing works selected from one form or from one broad or specific medium. The rules in AACR 2 are again much fuller, but both codes produce much the same broad result for treatment of form selections:

Bach, Johann Sebastian
[Cantatas. Selections]

IAML 3 does not specify in the main rules what to do with a selection of works for one medium of performance, whether broad or specific. AACR 2 has a sequence of rules (25.36A-C) which results in entries such as:

Handel, George Frideric
[Keyboard music. Selections]
Handel, George Frideric
[Organ music. Selections]

If the collection is complete in one medium (AACR 2) or in one form (both codes), the word 'selections' is dropped:

Wagner, Richard
[Operas]
Schoenberg, Arnold
[Vocal music]

IAML 3 has a footnote to rule 2.452 which says:

> When medium of performance is used as an identifying element for single works, it is retained for collections.

This presumably ties into the footnote alternative to rule 2.412 already referred to (p 42) rather than to the situation provided for in the main sequence of rules, when no thematic index or opus number is available (rule 2.413). It still does not provide for collections of a composer's music in one medium of performance, irrespective of form, as in the Handel examples above, but only for complete collections or selections of items such as piano sonatas or violin concertos, which result in headings such as:

Mozart, Wolfgang Amadeus
[Concertos. Piano & Orchestra]
Schubert, Franz
[Sonatas. Piano]

It may be trying to avoid the danger of a double sequence, almost a cross classification, which occurs in AACR 2, when entries under a prolific composer might occur for both form and medium. In fact examples are given in AACR 2 under medium:

[String quartet music]

and under form:

[Quartets, strings]

which perhaps underline the dangers of cross classification which IAML 3 is seeking to avoid. It would be perfectly possible to use the filing title:

[Works. Selections]

for a collection of (say) Bach's keyboard works which cut across various forms. This would be allowed by analogy with rule 2.4521 in IAML 3.

AACR 2 (rule 25.35) provides for selections which cut across both forms and mediums by using 'Selections' directly under the composer heading:

Dvořak, Antonin
[Selections; arr]
First year Dvorak

IAML 3 deals with this kind of work in the section on works of personal authorship. Rule 1.113 *Three or more works* [by the same composer]:

Enter under the name of the
composer
Beethoven, Ludwig Van
First year Beethoven

It would seem that to enter such works as AACR 2 does is to lose them. Are they not examples of distinctive titles to be entered in accordance with rule 25.27A? Even the example quoted under rule 25.35, ie Brahms (simplified), is distinctive although it starts with the name of the composer. Thus the uniform or filing title, using either code, would be:

Dvořak, Antonin
[First year Dvořak. . .]

IAML 3 probably intends the use of its rule for distinctive titles (2.421) for such selections.

Returning to AACR 2's system of uniform titles, observation of this can mean that entries in a catalogue for a single work may be scattered throughout the composer's entries according to the form or medium and/or the kind of publication. Thus Beethoven's *piano sonata no 22 in F major*, op 54 might appear under the following headings:

[Instrumental music]
[Keyboard music]
[Piano music]

[Selections]
[Sonatas]
[Sonatas, piano, no 22, op. 54, F major]
[Works]

If the library happens not to have a separate copy, an enquirer could be very puzzled and uncertain where to look without very full explanations and cross references. This is a very difficult problem of arrangement of entries, which is of course particularly acute for more prolific composers. AACR 1 (British text) had much the same system, but the North American text provided an alphabetico-classed arrangement giving the sequence:

[Sonata, piano, no 22, op 54, F major]
[Sonatas]
[Works]
[Works, instrumental]
[Works, keyboard]
[Works, piano]
[Works, selections]

In its interpretation of this, LC files uniform titles under a composer, so that the general collections are filed before the individual works. This has the effect of breaking the alphabetical sequence, but is more logical:

[Works]
[Works. Selections]
[Works, keyboard. Selections]
[Works, oboe]
[Concertos]
[Concerto, violin no 1]
[Sonatas, piano. Selections]
[Sonatas, piano, no 1]
etc.

This is slightly better in that the number of primary terms is reduced by subsuming some subdivisions under *Works*. Collections of sonatas could equally well be treated in the same way to give:

[Works. Sonatas]

This is possibly more logical than the sequence AACR 1 gives:

[Sonata, piano, no 22 . . .]
[Sonatas, piano]

which puts the single work before the collection. This particular discrepancy has now been corrected, of course, by the use of the plural form for the single work. The order of items on the shelves, if all a composer's works are brought together, would logically be:

Complete works
Selections of various kinds
Individual works

In practice, as has been pointed out in volume one, it is unlikely that this would happen, as the varying physical format of music makes this arrangement almost impossible to achieve on the shelves, and probably undesirable anyway. The question really is whether this logical arrangement is desired in the catalogue. AACR 2 is following, for music, the general pattern laid down in rules 25.8 to 25.11, but it is easier to arrange books on the shelves in the logical order referred to above, so at least such a classified arrangement under author will be found in one place (ie on the shelves) in the library with an alternative alphabetical approach in the catalogue.

If a library uses a classified catalogue, then it is likely that entry of titles in the classified file will be under medium of performance, so that an enquirer seeking a composer's works for (say) violin will find them brought together in the classified sequence, provided the search was initiated there, or via the subject or form index under:

Violin : music

Collocation of a composer's music for a particular medium will occur in the classified file whatever the uniform title may be, except where collected editions are classified together as in LC, or miniature scores similarly as in DC. In a dictionary catalogue, works for a particular medium would be similarly collocated by such headings as:

Violin music

But if an enquirer begins a search under the composer's name in either form of catalogue, then he or she will be faced by a sequence having a rather confused arrangement of entries if the search is for a prolific composer's works and AACR 2's system has been used to organize the entries. IAML 3's system is not the perfect solution, but it results in a simpler arrangement. It is perhaps an example of a situation where the old adage 'as simple as ABC' does not apply.

One possible solution is to admit defeat on the aim of using an alphabetical sequence for uniform titles under a composer's name, and have an initial sequence for complete works and selections under each composer, before the alphabetical sequence for individual works begins. This is suggested in IAML 2 (pp 39-40), where it is primarily intended for use in catalogues not employing uniform or filing titles:

If the conventional title system is not adopted, whose interest is primarily to permit a strict alphabetical arrangement without grouping works by instrument or type, it will be necessary, in filing the cards, to bring together the different editions of the same works. A systematic arrangement should be established for composers having an important body of work. It is not possible to give a unique model of arrangement applicable to all composers. We suggest making 5 sections but the system of arrangement must be adapted in each case to the nature of the production of the author:

Theatrical works
Vocal works
Instrumental works
Pedagogical works
Cross references.

Such a classified system could be used to cover the various kinds of complete and selected work eg:

1 Complete works
2 General selections
3 Instrumental music–Complete
4 Instrumental music–Selections
5 Vocal music–Complete
6 Vocal music–Selections
7 Individual works A-Z

Subdivisions under each heading would be by form, using the IAML 3 filing title consisting of entry under form for selections. This system is only suggested for composers for whom a library has a large number of entries in its catalogue. It means that under such a composer there would need to be an explanation of the arrangement at the beginning of the sequence. Then the series of guide cards or superimposed headings in a printed catalogue would display the sequence of broad heads, with appropriate entries appearing underneath them, arranged in alphabetical order by the filing title. Thus a sequence under Beethoven might be

Beethoven, Ludwig Van
4 Instrumental Music–Selections
Beethoven, Ludwig Van
[Sonatas. Selections]
Beethoven, Ludwig Van
[Symphonies, Selections]
etc.

As IAML 2 points out, such a system would have to be adapted to the needs of each composer, but it might well provide the user with a better view of the sequence. It is suggested with extreme reluctance, as it does mean the introduction of a different arrangement into an alphabetical sequence. The use of an arithmetical or decimal system does provide an alternative guide line, once the alphabetical sequence is broken.

Another solution also comes in the section on analytical entries in IAML 3. Rule 3.81 reads in part:

> Analytical entry may be made for a bibliographically independent work which is part of a series or a set of works. The cataloguing of such works is done according to the [rules for entry of individual works]. If the work is part of an edition of the collected works of a composer [or selections?] replace the series statement with a citation of the entry for the comprehensive work. . .

The example shows plainly how this should be done:

> Monteverdi, Claudio
> [Orfeo]
> Orfeo. Favola in musica. . .
> (Monteverdi, Claudio. [Works] Tutte le opere. Vol 11)

AACR 2 has a series of rules 13.4-13.6 which allows for a similar kind of entry. The use of analytical entries is of course very costly and their production is very time consuming. It is also obvious that they still leave the same system of main entries to which they refer. However, their use does help the reader looking for an individual work to be guided to all copies to be found in a library, whether they come as separate publications or as part of a larger edition.

Additional rules in AACR 2

Comment has been made throughout this chapter on the fact that AACR 2 provides many more rules than IAML 3. This does not necessarily make it better; a cataloguer coping with music titles might feel confused by too many rules. However, there are a number of rules for uniform titles in AACR 2 that do not have their counterpart in IAML 3's rules for filing titles.

Conflicting titles

There are a number of cases with distinctive titles when it may be necessary to distinguish between two works by the same composer bearing the same title. This situation occurs when a work originally written for one medium has been transcribed for another, for example Elgar's own piano transcription of the *Enigma variations*. It is necessary then to provide some further identifying element to each title according to rule 25.31B1:

[Variations on an original theme, orchestra]
[Variations on an original theme, piano]

The code seems rather confusing in its examples. The above example uses mediums of performance as identifying elements, but the rule also allows the use of a descriptive word or phrase in parentheses:

[Goyescas (Opera)]
[Goyescas (Piano work)]

It is difficult to see why this distinction is made:

Goyescas, opera
Goyescas, piano

distinguishes equally clearly and makes for greater consistency in layout. It may be a matter of punctuation really. Using IAML 3's method of punctuation results in:

[Goyescas. Opera]
[Goyescas. Piano]
[Variations on an original theme. Orchestra]
[Variations on an original theme. Piano]

Perhaps that is why IAML 3 provides no rule.

Arrangements

These are identified quite simply by adding the abbreviation *arr.* to the end of the uniform title [rule 25.31B2]:

Mendelssohn-Bartholdy, Felix
[Ein Sommernachtstraum. Scherzo; arr.]
Scherzo from A midsummer night's dream opus no 61, arranged for brass band . . .

When the arrangement is in the form of a vocal or chorus score, these terms are added as appropriate to the uniform title (rule 25.31B3):

Haydn, Joseph
[Die Schöpfung. Vocal score . . .]

For further comments on this see p 78. Rule 25.31B2 provides for similar treatment for librettos or song texts when these are published without music. Similar provision is made for the indication of the language of a text when appropriate:

Haydn, Joseph
[Die Schöpfung. Vocal score. English]

Relationship with general rules for uniform titles (AACR 2)

The speical rules for music uniform titles in AACR 2 are virtually complete in themselves, but the instruction at the beginning of the music section is to 'use the general rules 25.1-25.7 insofar as they apply to music and are not contradicted by [the rules for music]'. Reference is made here, therefore, only to those general rules which do not relate apparently to any rule for music, and to those on which it is felt some comment can usefully be made. Many of the music rules are in fact extensions of general rules to make them easily applicable to music.

Works created after 1500

There is a difference between the general rules and the corresponding music rule here. The general rule stipulates use of the title in the original language by which the work has become known through use in manifestations of the work or in reference sources (rule 25.3A). For music, the instruction is to use the composer's original title in the language in which it was formulated. Comment has already been made on the difficulties likely to be encountered in applying this rule, particularly in smaller libraries (p 34). It is difficult to see why the general rule wording could not have applied equally to music, especially as Mozart's *Don Giovanni* is used as an example under the general rule. Fortunately, it does not contradict the music rule.

Works created before 1501

There appears to be no equivalent rule for music. The general rule basically requires use of the original language title by which the work is identified in modern reference sources. There would seem to be no particular difficulty in applying this rule as most works are well documented in reference sources. RISM is obviously the most useful source of such information for music. It is to be hoped that it will be widely used in this way, in order to achieve easier interchange of information.

Parts of a work

The general rule (25.6A1) produces the completely opposite result to that obtained by applying the rule for music, ie the general rule requires use of the title of the part rather than that of the main work. The distinction made here means that all opera arias are collected under the title of the opera, instead of being separated under their own title or first line as they would be if the general rule were applied. There is a real distinction between music titles and other works. More often than not they are either derived from the first lines of arias or songs or from the tempo marking for a movement:

Voi che sapete
Allegro

To follow the general rule in this case would not be impossible for the first example, but would be pointless for the second. It is probably wise, however, to do as the code has done and make the different approach apply to all music.

It is perhaps useful to conclude this short section with a reminder of the point already made in describing AACR 2 (p 11), that, before the familiarity with its layout which comes with constant use is achieved, it is important to check the general rules as well as the particular rules for music. This applies equally to uniform titles, although the music rules are so full.

Rules for other materials

There are one or two cases where rules created for other materials might well apply to music; it is equally important for the music librarian to be aware of these rules, as libraries are constantly increasing the range of materials they use.

Composite manuscripts and manuscript groups

In this rule (25.13) a series of preferences for the source of the title is prescribed. They follow a logical order and their application to music produces such headings as:

Fitzwilliam virginal book
British Library. Manuscript Additional 299996.

without difficulty. The second refers to a collection of sixteenth century organ music with no particular title or fame. It is important to remember that this rule should be used for printed editions of the text and facsimile editions as well as for subject headings for analytical texts etc. It may be necessary to make analytical entries also for the composers of the works presented in the text.

Liturgical works

This could be a very important section of the code for many music libraries. The concern here is not settings of the mass by individual composers, which are obviously entered under the name of the composer, but official liturgies. It is not proposed to discuss this section further here. The code rules are very full and a number of references on p 469 of the code provide useful further guidance on how to proceed.

IAML 3 (rule 2.424) prescribes the use of the title in the official language of the church when the liturgy is official. An alternative footnote rule allows use of the language of the cataloguing library. The alternative gives

[Mass for peace]

rather than

[Missa pro pace]

The IAML 3 main rule produces broadly the same result as AACR 2, but is solely concerned with the music. AACR 2 is concerned with all aspects.

Conclusion

The treatment of uniform titles has received very full treatment by recent codes, but even now there is some doubt as to whether their full implications have been worked out. The examples in some sections of this chapter give cause for concern that, particularly in the case of AACR 2, they may result in separation of those items which it would be useful to bring together. Further there is a possible danger that they may confuse by introducing an artificial element between the composer heading and the title as it is copied from the title page or other source.

Nevertheless, it is important to remember that they do solve many of the problems to which reference was made in chapter one. Perhaps the main problem is that the actual purpose of the uniform title has not always been carefully distinguished in the formulation of rules. Until the appearance of IAML 3 and AACR 2 there appeared to be three basic reasons for prescribing uniform titles:

1 To bring together in a catalogue all entries for a work, however it may be designated on the title page or other source of information in the item being catalogued.

2 To assist in the filing of titles so that a logical order may be established for entries under an author or composer.

3 To provide information about the work being catalogued.

AACR 1 prescribed a fairly full uniform title giving the fullest information possible including any popular title by which the work is known, even when that title was not given by the composer, eg the 'London' in Haydn's 'London' symphony as compared with that in Vaughan Williams's *London symphony*. AACR2 has reduced this element considerably, while for IAML 3 this purpose has very little significance at all. This is all to the good. The purpose of a catalgoue is to provide information about a library's holdings, not to serve as a reference tool. In any case, it is more than likely that a great deal of this information will be provided in the transcript of the title found in the item. A further advantage of the reduction in information is that it lessens the dangers of errors in filing and the confusion that can arise from having too much information.

The rules in IAML 3 and the fact that it uses the term *filing title* indicate fairly clearly that it sees the second purpose as the most significant. Further, by its preference for use of the thematic index or opus number as the primary filing element immediately after the title, in the case of generic titles such as sonata, symphony etc, it achieves the first purpose fairly simply as well. The number of thematic catalogues is increasing, and collocation by such numbers, widely used in references to the music they represent, simplifies the whole process of definition of a work and the bringing together by the cataloguer of all its manifestations in print or otherwise. Filing by such numbers is a simple process. There are more problems with some composer's opus numbers, but, as long as consistency is maintained in the catalogue and the cataloguer is aware of the existence of the problems, they are important and useful secondary means of arrangement.

The difference in approach to this question of filing between IAML 3 and AACR 2 hinges partly on the fact that the IAML Cataloguing Commission had constantly to remember that it was trying to produce a code which would be a satisfactory basis for international co-operation between different language groups. The difference is also another expression of the debate about the relative merits of alphabetical and numerical filing, which has long vexed classificationists in devising notation for classification schemes. It is possibly a dispute which can never be resolved, as there are probably as many persons who find one method easier as there are those who are proponents of the other.

The relative merits of the two systems are difficult to resolve in the present context, except that the evidence seems to be that the IAML committee has produced a more consistent filing system, in that under all circumstances the numbers, when they exist, are preferred to anything else. AACR 2 does use numbers when available, but in cases where the medium of performance is not implied in the title (eg it is in symphonies, but not in concertos), the medium has priority over all else unless it is complex. There must be inconsistencies here, whichever method is used, because not all composers have thematic or opus numbering systems, but AACR 2 adds inconsistency under a composer like Mozart who has a universally recognized thematic catalogue. It is perhaps a small point, but the user of a catalogue must always be considered, as must the assistant who files items into the sequence. The simpler the uniform title is, the easier is the manipulation of the catalogue, whether the agent is a human being or a computer.

Perhaps the ultimate test is that it is easier to write instructions on filing and use of the catalogue following the IAML 3 system than it is following that observed in AACR 2. Having said all this, it remains good advice to smaller libraries to use the AACR 2 system:

[Concertos, piano]

[Sonatas, violin, piano]

Filing is less of a problem in a smaller catalogue anyway, and the first purpose of uniform titles can be given total priority. Such usage is much more likely to be appreciated in a library serving, for the most part, the non-specialist user.

The first aim in devizing uniform titles, that of collocation, is achieved for the most part by both codes, except for the separation of copies of a work which are included in complete editions, selections etc. This has already been discussed fully and solutions offered. The emphasis in AACR 2 seems to be more on this purpose for uniform titles. The introduction to the relevant section states:

> Uniform titles provides the means for bringing together all the catalogue entries for a work when various manifestations . . . of it have appeared under various titles. . .

Both codes allow discretion in the use of uniform titles. AACR 2 allows their application according to the policy of the cataloguing agency. IAML 3 (rule 2.2) says they are to be used:

> . . . when a work is published with titles in a language other than that of the first edition, or varying from that of the first edition; when a composer has written more than one work having the same title; or when the publication consists of an excerpt from a larger work

Consistency suggests that they should be used all the time, especially as an aid to filing. However, it does look rather silly to have an entry reading:

Alwyn, William
    [Symphony no 1]
    Symphony no 1

The use of square brackets indicates quite clearly when a contrived title has been inserted, so in such cases there seems little point in putting the uniform title there.

Alwyn, William
Symphony no 1

is in fact the title of the first edition, the uniform title and the filing title expressed in one. Another possiblilty of course is to use the uniform title all the time and not bother to even give the title as it appears in the work being catalogued. In many libraries the user is only concerned to establish from the catalogue that the library has a particular item. If the uniform title identifies the work correctly, such an enquirer is not interested in knowing what is on the title page. It may be necessary in these circumstances to return to giving additional identifying information in the uniform title, which under IAML 3's and AACR 2's systems could only be gained from the item's own title, eg:

Josephs, Wilfred
Symphony no 5 op 75, 'Pastoral'

rather than

Josephs, Wilfred
Symphony. Op 75.

The latter entry follows IAML 3 correctly. The former gives fuller information gleaned from the title page which reads:

Pastoral symphony/no 5. Opus 75.

Uniform or filing titles remain a useful device for solving a number of problems met with in cataloguing music. Used with care and discretion they will assist greatly in the systematic organization of entries under a composer's name. The following rules for their use have been developed for the music libraries of the University of Cambridge. They are offered here as a useful guide, and summary of the basic processes in forming uniform titles:

NOMENCLATURE

The term Uniform title is adopted as a general name.
(Abbreviation: UT)

Two types of UT can be distinguished:
Conventional title (abbreviation: CT)
Original title (abbreviation: OT)

Two types of UT

The title of a work is defined as the name which distinguishes the work, exclusive of any statement of medium or key, of serial, opus or thematic index number, of ordinal or cardinal number, of date of composition, laudatory adjective or fanciful or descriptive epithet unless attached to the work by the composer. In the following examples titles as here defined are in italics:

Grand *sonata* in B♭ op. 32
Mozart's favourite *minuet*
String *quartet* Hob III.19
Troisième *nocturne*
Five *flower songs*

Vespers (1610)
Symphony no. 40
Sechs *Hölderlin Fragmente*
Moonlight *sonata*
Symphonie fantastique

Titles as so defined will usually fall into one of two categories, *viz.*

Generic titles: those titles which simply indicate a musical form or genre, eg fugue, sonata, quartet, symphony.

Distinctive titles: those titles which in themselves absolutely distinguish the work, *eg* Aïda, Images, Album für die Jugend. Distinctive titles may include the name of a musical form or genre, *eg* Symphonie fantastique.

For generic titles, use CT's.

For distinctive titles, use OT's.

Formulation and language of UT

Conventional titles. The name and language of the form or genre most commonly known in England should be adopted, eg sonata, not sonate, quintet, not quintett, quintette or quintetto.*

Original titles. The form and language of the title of the first published works, the title authorized by the composer should be adopted. If either of these is impossible to ascertain, the form and language most commonly accepted internationally may be adopted.

TRANSLITERATION AND ROMANIZATION

Titles in non-roman alphabets should be transliterated.

Titles in non-alphabetic languages should be romanized.

*Note that an English equivalent is not necessarily the most suitable, especially if a foreign term gives more precision, eg étude may be preferred to study, Lied to song.

CHAPTER THREE

DESCRIPTION

THE DESCRIPTIVE element of cataloguing is perhaps the central aspect of the whole process. Certainly the art of describing manuscripts and early printed books has been raised to such a high standard of analysis and accuracy that it is possible to visualise the complete physical construction of an item, as well as details of its publishing history and much else besides, from a full cataloguing entry. Much the same type of approach has been applied to later publications, and, for example, specialist catalogues of some modern authors have been prepared with the same painstaking eye to detail. The only difference is that modern printing is very much a mechanical process and therefore it is not usually possible to identify individual copies of an edition as it is in describing books published in the early days of printing, when, for example, among other causes for variation, an author might sit by the press and make alterations as the pages were printed so that there would be differences between earlier and later copies within the same edition. Some modern editions have each copy numbered, especially when they have been produced on a hand press, and it is obviously possible to identify them individually.

Cataloguers of early music have learned much from the researches of their colleagues in the book world, and some very detailed catalogues of early music have been published. Some aspects of this work are discussed later in this chapter and a few examples of catalogues of early music are cited in the bibliography. However, there does not always seem to have been the same attention to detail by cataloguers of music, particularly in the cataloguing of more modern works. Thematic catalogues, for example, have been mainly concerned with indicating where an autograph manuscript may be found and giving some account of its provenance when this is known, rather than with trying to describe its physical nature in detail. This is equally true of their references to early printed editions of a composer's works. Of course the use of a theme identifies the work, but the inclusion of music, even if only brief, in a printed catalogue considerably increases the cost of producing such a catalogue, so the use of themes in library catalogues, for example, has not become very widespread. For accounts of the development of thematic catalogues, see the introduction to the book by Barry Brook (Brook 1972) and the article by Lenore Coral (Coral 1973).

It is interesting to consider the nature of the creation which music catalogues are attempting to describe. Music has at least a double rôle once it has been written down or printed. It exists as both sound and the representation of that sound in print. Nowadays, of course, the first physical presentation of that sound may be in a commercially issued recording or in a private recording made for a radio station's sound archive. This may be the first published edition of a work and could constitute a more authoritative representation of what the composer wanted than the first printed edition. Musical notation is a very imperfect method of representing sound, and all kinds of nuances which it is impossible to represent in a printed score may be heard in a recording. The latter naturally assumes particular importance if the composer has conducted or played in the recorded performance. Bartók, for example, gave very precise timings for his works in the printed score, but there are variations on these in some of his recorded performances. These are by no means wide variations, but do indicate that a performance may vary according to mood rather more than the precision of the printed score might suggest.

Jazz is a style of music in which recordings assume major importance. Duke Ellington is a composer whose works exist for the most part on record and not in score form. His *Black, brown and beige suite* has been superbly reconstructed, partially from an incomplete printed score, but mainly from recordings of the works. The full details of how this was done can be found in the sleeve notes to the reconstruction by the Alan Cohen Band (Argo ZDA 159). Comparison is possible with the Ellington version on RCA LSA 3071.

All music must be performed in order to be realized, unless it is considered in the very abstract sense. When an author writes a book the contact with readers is immediate. For listeners, there has to be the intermediary performance of music, which immediately introduces the question of interpretation. Indeed, performance may radically alter the structure of a work, and the first printed edition may consequently be a copy of a recording rather than of the autograph manuscript. In such circumstances, the latter has less importance–has indeed become misleading—as a representation of what the composer intends. It retains its value, however, as a guide to the composer's first intentions. Such has been the power of the printed word that there is still a tendency on the part of many to feel that in any dispute print must represent the truth, but the foregoing illustrates very clearly that this is not always so.

The nature of a performance is relatively easy to establish when a recording of it exists, but obviously not so easy when it comes to establishing the true text of a work by Monteverdi or Bach or their contemporaries. The attempt to ascertain what the composer wanted in these circumstances calls for accuracy of detail, painstaking research and considerable imagination on the part of musicologists, who are generally responsible for preparing modern printed editions of early works for the press. It is important, therefore, that bibliographers and librarians provide accurate information in catalogues and bibliographies, so that their description of items may leave the musicologist in no doubt. To request a microfilm copy of a work is less expensive than to travel many miles to a library to see it, but it remains time consuming and by no means cheap. Not all libraries are quick in supplying copies; it is doubly frustrating to discover that the item expected with such patience is useless or not the item the catalogue apparently claimed it to be.

Description in catalogues is therefore a valuable process which needs to be completed with care and attention to detail. However, the descriptive element needs to be manipulated to accord with the level of enquiry which users of a library are going to make. In many libraries readers, if they bother to go to the catalogue at all, will look at an entry and record the name of the composer, the title and the class number, which indicates where the item may be found. This is the extreme opposite in use to that anticipated for the kind of description discussed earlier. The sole function of the catalogue in these circumstances is to serve as a finding guide. It answers the question:

Where may I find this peice of music?

Charles Amni Cutter, who can justly be described as the father of modern cataloguing, stated the following purposes for a catalogue (Cutter 1904):

(i) To enable a person to find a document of which
- (a) the author, or)
- (b) the title, or) is known
- (c) the subject)

(ii) To show what the library has
  (d) by a given author
  (e) on a given subject (and related subjects)
  (f) in a given kind (or form) of literature
(iii) To assist in the choice of a document
  (g) as to its edition (bibliographically)
  (h) as to its character (literary or topical)

Certainly most enquiries in many libraries come in the first three of Cutter's categories and require the minimum description. His next three objectives cover the collocative function of catalogues, served as far as authors and composers are concerned by ensuring that all their works are brought together in a catalogue under the same heading. The last two aims are served partly by the uniform title and partly by the bibliographical description of an item. The amount of that description must vary according to the purpose and function of the library, to which a catalogue serves as a guide. The needs of users must dictate the level of description. To provide information which is never used is a waste of time and money. It is easy to justify excessive detail by pointing to occasional use, but that really will not do. Occasional demand for certain information such as place of printing or the address of the publisher can nearly always be satisfied by reference to published bibliographies and catalogues.

Catalogue codes in the past have usually aimed at providing for the level of description appropriate for research libraries. A welcome change between AACR 1 and AACR 2 can be clearly noted. The effect of this different approach is immediately apparent in the section on description in the new code, where three levels of descriptive cataloguing are permitted (rule 1.0D). Even the third level, which is the fullest, allows discretion according to the kind of document being catalogued, while the first is almost so brief as to equate with the very frequent question:

Have you got this title by this author?

IAML 3, being a code for full cataloguing, is prevented by its very purpose from providing rules for the restriction of the description. Surprisingly, IAML 2, a code for limited cataloguing, does not apparently do this either.

Description in cataloguing is now generally accepted as beginning with the title proper (ie as it appears in the item being catalogued). The heading for the entry is the means by which the description is located in the catalogue, while the uniform title, as has been suggested, is accepted now as serving principally a double rôle of filing and collocating. It does not normally add to the description of an item, as that should be based on the item itself; although, certainly in the case of music, it may correct some information which the item being catalogued contains (eg incorrect opus or serial number), in order to ensure that the entry for the item is filed in its correct and most useful place in the catalogue. The uniform title is organized in a predetermined way according to rules which are provided, whereas the descriptive part of an entry must describe a document as it is and not as the cataloguer might desire it to be.

Parts of a description

These together with their purpose are:

1 *Title* This should include the title as presented in the publication together with any sub-title or alternative title.

2 *Author statement* This is frequently only given nowadays in library catalogues if the form of name differs from that used for the author in the heading, or if entry has been made under some heading other than the author's name, or where there are several authors and only one has been named in the heading. In full cataloguing it will be necessary to give the author's name even when it is in the same form as that used for the heading.

3 *Edition statement* Used to identify a revision or an edition other than the first. It is not usual to indicate a further printing or impression of the same edition.

4 *Imprint* The purpose here is to identify the place of publication, publisher and date of publication of the edition in hand. Publication history, if required, is given in a note. For recordings it is usual to give the name of the series rather than the main company (eg Archive, not Polydor or DGG).

5 *Collation* This describes the physical makeup of the item. For a book this means the number of volumes, if more than one, or the number of pages and plates, if this is only one volume, followed by details of the illustrations and the height. The collation of other forms will give corresponding information eg for a recorded item the number of sides of a disc occupied by the item, the speed at which the disc plays and the number of sound channels (mono, stereo etc).

6 *Series statement* This provides details of any larger series of publications of which the item catalogued forms a part eg Great tenors of the past; Master musicians etc.

7 *Notes* These give any additional bibliographical information which is felt to be necessary eg the instrumentation in the case of a set of orchestral scores and parts. They may further include full details of contents when an item includes several works eg a recording of a number of songs.

The layout of a full catalogue entry providing all the above information varies from catalogue to catalogue and is likely to be affected by the physical format used for the catalogue. Nevertheless, the following is fairly typical of contemporary cataloguing style (heading, uniform title and class number are shown for the sake of completeness):

Heading Class number
[Uniform title]
Title statement. Author statement (if needed)
Edition statement. Imprint
Collation. (Series statement)
Notes

This entry, it should be understood, has not been affected by any international standards or computerization as far as punctuation etc is concerned. It merely attempts to show what the average entry should contain if reasonable completeness is the intention. Demonstrated on a typical musical example, the title page of which reads:

Hawkes pocket scores/Benjamin Britten/Concerto/for piano and orchestra/op. 13/Boosey & Hawkes/Music Publishers Limited/ London–Paris–Rome–Johannesburg–Sydney–Toronto–New York/Made in England Net Price

the layout appears in the form

Britten, Benjamin MPQF
[Concerto, piano, orchestra, op. 13]
Concerto for piano and orchestra op 13.
London : Boosey & Hawkes, 1967.
178p. 19 cm. (Hawkes pocket scores)
Miniature score.

The class number shown is assigned from the BCM scheme. The date is given on the first page of the score. Other information which might be added to the entry is discussed below, when the particular problems of music cataloguing in relation to description are examined.

This entry can of course be shortened according to the use made of a particular library. It could, for example, be shortened to:

Britten, Benjamin MPQF
[Concerto, piano, orchestra, op. 13]

Concerto for piano and orchestra op 13.
Boosey & Hawkes (Hawkes pocket scores)

without losing any really vital information. Even briefer:

Britten MPQF
Concerto, piano, orchestra, op. 13
(Hawkes pocket score)

For some cataloguers there may almost be heresy preached in such an idea, but cataloguing processes must not exceed the known need. The tail must not wag the dog.

International standards

The splendid work of IFLA in producing the various ISBDs cannot be praised too highly. Such an enterprise can only serve to assist users of libraries in all countries. If it means a certain amount of adaptation to different forms of entry from those to which we have all become accustomed, such as the one exemplified above, then this is a price surely worth paying. ISBDs can only help to make the interchange of information between countries easier. This must benefit music librarians perhaps more than most given the international nature of music.

ISBDs are not intended to be used as cataloguing codes, but form the organizational basis for description on which national codes can be constructed. ISBD (G) is the fundamental standard on which all other ISBDs are based and they all require the descriptive information in catalogue entries to be organized in the same way. The ISBD for non book materials including recordings, ISBD (NBM), is published, but the one for printed music, ISBD (PM), does not appear until later this year (1979). AACR 2 is based for its rules for description on the relevant ISBD, but IAML 3 had appeared before the ISBDs were developed. IAML 3 is, of course, itself aimed at providing an international cataloguing standard for music. Further, the committee responsible for ISBD (PM) is a joint one representing both IAML and IFLA. There must obviously be changes in punctuation and layout, but it is likely that apart from that the basic rules of IAML 3 on description will still be valid or easily adapted when necessary.

The specified areas of description in the various ISBDs all refer to that in ISBD (G) which is as follows:

1 Title and statement of responsibility area
2 Edition area
3 Material (or type of publication) specific area

4 Publication, distribution etc area
5 Physical description area
6 Series area
7 Note area
8 Standard number (or alternative) and terms of availability area

As can be seen, these conform broadly with the items referred to above (p 65) as representing the normal description in an average catalogue. The three new terms are *statement of responsibility, material specific area* and *standard number.* In addition under area 1 there appears *general material designation.*

Statement of responsibility. This is a statement which identifies the person(s) or corporate body who are responsible for the creation of the artistic or intellectual content of a work, whether in part or a whole. In the example used earlier in this chapter the statement of responsibility is 'Benjamin Britten'.

Material (or type of publication) specific area. This is not used by many ISBDs. It refers to the designation of the specific class of material to which an item belongs. It is not used by either ISBD (NBM) or ISBD (PM) in its final draft form. It is used in the ISBD (CM) for mathematical data–scale projection etc.

General material designation. This refers to a term defining broadly the class to which an item belongs. It is normally placed immediately after the title proper eg following ISBD (NBM) the general material designation, use of which is optional, appears in the form:
Dido and Aeneas [Sound recording]
La traviata [Motion picture]

Standard number. This refers to the ISBN or International standard book number, which identifies an edition of a work issued by one specific publisher and is unique to that edition. Thus the ISBN for volume 1 of this work was 0-85157-231-6 UK (0-208-01544-2 in the USA). There is a similar system for serials (ISSN) but unfortunately not as yet for music or sound recordings.

Particular problems in describing printed music (Sound recordings are treated separately below. See p 84)

Music comes in a variety of forms and from many countries. Those two facts in themselves present problems. It will be necessary to distinguish the kind of score and also to cope with title pages in a number of languages and in different alphabets.

Title

IAML 3 (rule 3.11) prescribes the sources of information for the description of a work as the title page, cover title or caption title in that order of preference. AACR 2 (rule 5.0B1) has a similar list, but reverses caption and cover and adds colophon, other preliminaries and other sources. When the title of the particular publication is one in a long list (passepartout) then both codes prescribe using only the information germane to the item being catalogued. The ISBD (PM) is likely to follow a similar pattern, except that once the title page has failed as a prime source of information, the cataloguer is to be allowed discretion between the cover or the first page of music.

Chapter one referred to the lack of title pages on a lot of music. It is therefore particularly important that adequate guidance is given on how to proceed in such circumstances. Perhaps the fact that IAML 3 and AACR 2 have different orders of preference between cover and caption underlines the difficulty of choice. The proposed order for ISBD (PM) is a compromise which recognizes this as an area which can be left to the discretion of a competent cataloguer.

Parallel titles are met more frequently in music than in most other areas of knowledge. The ISBD solution, adopted of course by AACR 2, prescribes that they be given connected by the equals sign = . This is a very simple and effective indication which scarcely needs interpretation:

Die Jahreszeiten [Printed music] = The seasons = Les saisons

IAML 3 prescribes that the first title is transcribed completely. For other languages only the title proper is to be given. If there are more than three languages, all after the third are to be omitted eg:

> Classical beginnings (light classical and romantic pieces) for pianoforte/classiques pour débutants (morceaux classiques et romantiques faciles) pour le piano/Klassische Musik für Anfänger (leichte klassische und romantische Stücke) für Klavier
> Selected and Edited with interpretative notes by /choisis et publiés avec notations par/ausgewählt und mit Erläuterungen versehen von/ Dorothy Bradley

would be transcribed as:

> Classical beginnings for pianoforte. Classiques pour débutants pour le piano. Klassische Musik für Anfänger für Klavier. (Light classical and romantic pieces), selected and edited by Dorothy Bradley.

AACR 2 (rule 1.1D2) approaches parallel titles slightly differently as far as choice is concerned, as it is an English based code. The first parallel title is given, then any subsequent one in English. The examples make it plain that three parallel titles are to be given. The rule seems to imply that the English parallel title should appear second, but the third example under 1.1D and the first under 5.1D1 indicate that this is not so. (See appendix 1)

AACR 2 (rule 5.1B2) requires the statement of medium of performance, the key and/or the opus number to be treated as part of the title proper if the title consists of a generic term:

Variations on folksongs Opp. 105, 107
for piano solo [Printed music]

otherwise it is treated as other title information and comes after the general material designation:

Lucifer [Printed music] Oratorio for solo
voice and orchestra.

When in doubt, such a statement is to be treated as part of the title proper.

This question of where to put such items does not occur with IAML 3, as it has no general material designation. Rule 3.122 does require such items to be added to the title if they do not appear in the source. This hardly seems necessary if the filing title supplies such information. Rule 5.1B3 in AACR 2 suggests that if a title has to be manufactured, the elements are to be given in the order prescribed for uniform titles.

IAML 3 has a rule (3.111) to cover the presence of more than one title page in an item. This rule allows for discretion between several possibilities eg: 1 The second of two pages facing each other, 2 The title page in the language of the text, etc. AACR 2 covers the same situation and more in a general rule (1.1B8). This gives first place to the title in the language of the text and then, if that is not available, the most appropriate according to layout. It is good to see both codes allowing discretion to the cataloguer in a number of areas of description. Publishers, particularly of music, produce such astonishingly varied title pages it would be quite impossible to cover all situations by rules.

While AACR 2 requires the title proper to be transcribed exactly, except for its punctuation and capitalization (rules 1.1B1 and 5.1B1), the elements of the whole title statement are to be recorded in the prescribed order even if that means tranposing data (rule 1.1A2). This is a change for the better from the practice of older codes which required all the title page information to be copied exactly, thereby producing inconsistency in catalogues.

Statements of responsibility

AACR 2 has a brief rule (5.1F including F1 and F2) in the music section, but care must be taken here to refer to the rules in the general section under 1.1F where much fuller treatment is given and most of the rules apply equally to music. Whether the statement of responsibility is recorded when it is the same as that used for the heading of the entry depends on the level of description used. The second and third levels require it in all circumstances.

Of the rules given in the section 1.1F the following are of particular interest:

Rule 1.1F2 makes it quite clear that, if there is no statement of responsibility prominent in the item, one is not to be made up. If it is felt necessary, then it is to be given in a note. It may well appear as the heading (eg rule 21.5B on known authors of anonymous works might well apply to the heading). 1.1F3 allows the statement of responsibility to be transposed if it comes before the title proper eg:

Beethoven/Klaviersonaten

is transcribed:

Klaviersonaten [Printed music] / Beethoven

Rule 1.1F6 covers the situation where there is more than one statement of responsiblitiy. The sequence on layout of the chief source of information is to be the guide here. Otherwise, very sensibly, the instruction is to follow the order which makes the most sense. Vocal music is almost certain to have two statements of responsibility. The vocal score of *Der Rosenkavalier* illustrates this:

Richard Strauss/Der Rosenkavalier/Le chevalier à la Rose/Kömodie für Musik in drei Aufzügen von Hugo von Hofmannsthal/Comedy for Music in three Acts by Hugo von Hofmannsthal/Comédie pour musique en trois actes par Hugo von Hofmannsthal

Rule 1.1F8 allows an explanatory word to be added to make a relationship between title and persons clear. 1.1E5 requires other title information to follow the title proper or parallel title to which it belongs. The description then transcribes as follows:

Der Rosenkavalier [Printed music] : Komödie für Musik in drei Aufzügen = Le chavalier à la rose : comédie pour musique en trois actes : comedy for music in three acts / von Hugo von Hofmannsthal; [Musik von] Richard Strauss

It could be decided that the other title information is too lengthy here (1.1E3), but it would be difficult to know what to omit other than the English phrase. Rule 1.1F11 states that the statement of responsibility is given in the language or script of the title proper, if it is not practicable to give it in each language represented in the parallel titles.

A statement of responsibility is to be transcribed even if no person or body is named (rule 1.1F14). This is likely to be fairly common in music with such phrases as eg:

Sixteen English folksongs [Printed music] / arranged for piano [Note : The code prefers [music] as the general material designation. I have followed the draft ISBD (PM) and used [Printed music] as this seems more precise. The ISBD (PM) will include rules for statement of responsibility to cover, for printed music, those problems set out in rules 1.1F to 1.1F15].

Editions

IAML 3 has a very brief rule requiring the last element in the title to be the edition statement. If the edition statement is found elsewhere than in the source of information for the title, it is to be included in square brackets.

AACR 2 has several rules which cover such matters as (1) edition statements in more than one language (5.2B4), when the language of the title proper is to be followed. The examples given for the IAML rule imply the same procedure. (2) Statements of responsibility relating to one or more editions but not all (5.2C1). These are to be recorded following the edition statement. 1.2C2 requires them to be given in the title and statement of responsibility area if there is a doubt. (3) Revisions of editions. These together with a statement of responsibility for them are to be recorded if significant. The rules under music are closely related to the general rules in this area and are basically only necessary to allow for musical examples. It would seem easier in such circumstances to have one set of rules and to give examples of different kinds of materials under them.

The draft ISBD (PM) suggests that when parallel edition statements appear, the one appearing first is to be given. Parallel statements may also be given. This appears to be the only proposal which differs from AACR 2's rules. An additional proposal relates to details of appendices applying to the edition being catalogued. It is proposed that they are to be given as statements of responsibility relating to the edition when they are found on the title page or title page substitute, or when a person or corporate body is named as responsible for them in a formal statement elsewhere in the publication. Otherwise, it is proposed that the details are given as part of the edition statement. When a person or corporate body is not clearly related to one edition, it is proposed that the statement be recorded in the title and statement of responsibility area. It is to be hoped that more examples will be given in the group of rules referring to appendices (2.3.2.), as their purpose is not entirely clear.

While the wording is somewhat different and slightly less clear in ISBD (PM), the effect is the same as that achieved by the rules in AACR 2. The edition statement in both cases is frequently a statement about the physical nature of the score based on the wording used in the score (AACR : 1.2B1, ISBD (PM) : 2.1.2.):

Partitur
Score and set of parts
2nd ed.
Vocal score

Both allow an edition statement to be added if the publication does not have one, when the cataloguer feels there is a significant difference between the item and other editions of the same work (AACR 2 : 5.2B3; ISBD (PM) : 2.1.2.). This is optional in both systems:

[Ed. for B_b clarinet]
[Urtext]

When the editorial work relates to all editions, the statement of responsibility comes in the title area:

The musical offering and three trio sonatas [Printed music] / J.S. Bach; from the Bach – Gesellschaft edition. – Score

The edition statement is preceded by. – in both systems.
The statement of responsibility relating to a particular edition is part of the edition statement:

L'infedelta delusa [Printed music] / Franz Joseph Haydn; edited by H.C. Robbins Landon . – Vocal score with English text by Andrew Porter

Imprint

IAML 3 requires only the first named place of publication to be given, unless another place is clearly the actual place of publication eg

London – LEIPZIG – New York

If there is more than one place, those other than the one named in the imprint are represented by etc. The same applies to publishers' names, except that two places and publishers are named if one of the later or less prominent names is in the country of the cataloguing library (rules 3.41 and 3.42). AACR 2 and ISBD (G) together with the draft ISBD (PM) have the same basic approach and additional rules to cover such situations as no publisher being named (the abbreviation [s.n.] for *sine nomine* is used) and the naming of an agent or distributor–a provision which is particularly useful for music. The rule comes in the general area of AACR 2 and in the ISBD (G) as well as in the ISBD (PM). Both codes and the ISBDs allow for the shortest form of name possible to be used, although the wording in IAML 3 implies slightly less freedom, merely allowing the omission of 'Co', 'Ltd', etc eg:

B. Schott's Söhne Mainz

Imprint . – Mainz : Schott

Munich/Henle/English agent Novello/London

Imprint . – Munich : Henle; London : Novello [agent]

Plate number

Rule 5.4D2 (AACR 2) refers the supplying of plate numbers to a note. There are some interesting variations on the location of this useful piece of information:

IAML 1	:	Imprint
IAML 2	:	Collation
IAML 3	:	Imprint
AACR 1	:	Imprint
AACR 2	:	Notes
ISBD (PM)	:	Standard number area

IAML 3 suggests the publisher's number as distinct from the plate number may be given as a series note, while ISBD (PM) places it with the standard number. For the latter, the publisher's number *must* be given, whereas statement of the plate number is optional. Whatever else it has done, this very useful piece of information has obviously caused the compilers of cataloguing regulations some trouble. Democratic procedure would imply the imprint as its proper home. Certainly it has more significance than its placing by AACR 2 suggests. It is a very useful means of identifying a particular edition; after all it is the method by which the publisher and the printer identify it to each other. It is very closely associated with the publisher's name, quite often having the publisher's initials preceding it:

B.S.S. 36283 [B. Schott's Söhne]

U.E. 9 [Universal Edition]

In the second of these two examples, this is also what is defined in codes as the publisher's number. It is much more a fundamental part of the work than the recording company's label number in the case of a disc, being more akin to the matrix number so widely used in discographies of early records. But then these two have also been relegated to notes by AACR 2. They all belong more logically to the imprint area. There is justification for the collation as the plate number is associated with printing, and for standard number as it could obviously be a part of any such number for music. But the relegation to notes by AACR 2 has no justification in view of the plate number's value. [In fairness it must be observed that this was a minority view on the Cataloguing Rules Subcommittee of IAML (UK) after a long discussion. The majority view, represented in AACR 2's rule, was quite rightly presented as the view of the committee.]

Date

The dating of music is a very problematic area. Much published music has no date at all, and it scarcely has significance with some kinds of publication. It is still possible to buy quite a range of music which was first published in the nineteenth century and has remained in print ever since. With publishers becoming more aware of the high cost of storage space, this practice is decreasing, particularly as the many small family music publishing firms are taken over by larger international enterprises which are much more cash conscious. With much of this kind of material it is impossible, and probably unimportant, to date it very precisely. The need to do so will depend very much on the kind of library and the needs of readers. In a very interesting paper given at the Manchester conference of the IAML (UK) Branch in 1977 Oliver Neighbour outlined some of the problems faced by the Music library of the British Library Reference Division in trying to date nineteenth century music. Among other items which can help when they are available, he suggested contemporary publishers' lists, thematic catalogues, contemporary newspapers and journals (particularly the advertisements), concert programmes, printing dates of the printing firm responsible etc. The problems of dating early music are fully covered in *Guide for dating early published music* compiled by Donald W Krummel under the auspices of IAML (London, Kassel : Bärenreiter; Hackensack, N J Boonin, 1974) with a supplement in *Fontes artis musicae* XXIV 1977/8, 175-184.

IAML 3 suggests using such sources as suggested above if the date is not given in the publication. Alternative dates to that of publication can obviously be the copyright, printing or legal deposit date. When the date is incorrect, the correct date can be supplied alongside if known. There are also a number of methods given for supplying uncertain dates. IAML 2 has much more information about dating, which is curious when the relationships of the two codes is considered. It suggests making considerable investigations which would be unlikely in the kind of library for which IAML 2 was envisaged. However, it is a useful survey of dating practice from the sixteenth century. Necessarily brief, it needs to be supplemented by use of Don Krummel's admirable guide and its supplement and also by reference to some of the books listed on page 25 of IAML 2.

AACR 2 has a number of rules in the general section under 1.4F which deal with various aspects of the problem. There is no difference from the practice outlined by IAML 2 and 3, but there are additional rules covering (1) dates given in calendars other than the Gregorian or Julian. For example:

5730 [1969 or 1970]

(2) When a re-issue date is given in the edition area, only the re-issue date is given in the imprint. (3) Distribution date and copyright date can be given in addition if known to be significantly different. The ISBDs have basically the same rules as AACR 2. All methods allow for the standard practice of dating works which have appeared or are appearing over a period of years:

1911-1915

1975-

Really the fundamental problem is not the way the date is expressed but finding the correct date to record. In the average library too much time should not be spent on this. The standard abbreviation for no date can be used ie [n.d.]. After the Universal Copyright Convention introduced from September 1955 the use of the © symbol, more music has become dateable accurately from the copyright notice.

The name of the printer together with place of printing may be given as an optional extra if AACR 2 and ISBD (PM) are used as guides. The deatils, using AACR 2, follow the basic imprint in parentheses:

London : Chappell, 1971 (London : Lowe & Brydone)

All the codes and the ISBD (PM) allow the use of the printers name if the publisher is unknown. The layout is quite different, however. IAML 2 gives none for any part of the imprint, saying it should follow the usage of the library, while IAML 3 has the form:

Norwich, Printed by J. Smith for the author, [1801?]

AACR 2 on the other hand requires:

[Norwich? : s.n., 1801?] (Norwich : J. Smith, printer)

Following IAML 3, the plate number is then given after the date preceded by the abbreviation 'Pl.no.'. It is only to be given when there is not date of publication or copyright in the work. Either here or immediately after the publisher's name is the most logical place for it to be given. It is a useful means of identification and there would be value in its inclusion irrespective of the presence of the date.

Collation (Physical description)

The information supplied in this area needs to be fairly flexible when music is being described. For monographs it is usual to give details of pagination, illustrations and size. AACR 2 prescribes the layout:

xi, 299 p. : maps, ports.; 24 cm.

4 v. : all ill.; 22 cm.

IAML 2 goes so far as to suggest, very sensibly for many libraries, that this part of the description can be omitted altogether. However, if a work published from approximately 1800 is issued in several parts, details would be recorded *in a note* without indicating the number of pages:

Score & 24 parts

However, in describing earlier music issued only in parts, more detail is to be given, using the exact name given in the publication. It is particularly important to indicate if any parts are missing:

Cantus 46p.; Altus 46p.; Tenor 50p.; the other parts are missing

IAML 3 (rules 3.51-3.53) prescribes the collation very much in the form AACR 2 requires for monographs, except that the punctuation is different. The use of such phrases as score, miniature score, etc is indicated:

[8], score (283 p) (Preliminary textual matter precedes the score)

This preliminary matter is on unnumbered pages. The number of parts should be recorded, and, as with IAML 2, more detail can be given in notes:

Score (35 p), 4 parts.

Score (2 v), 30 parts.

Illustrations can be described according to the rules for books. In some series of miniature scores it is customary to include a portrait of the composer. This scarcely seems important, but its presence can be indicated in accordance with IAML 3:

Miniature score (60 p. port)

Size is given as for books.

AACR 2 has a series of rules (5.5A-5.5E) which recognize the special physical nature of music. A full collation following AACR 2 would have the form:

1 score (35 p) : ill + 4 parts; 28 cm.

5.5B1 includes the specific material designation to indicate the kind of score. When different kinds are issued together they are to be listed in the order prescribed in the code. This gives different kinds of score in which all the parts are included first (eg condensed score), then piano or violin etc, conductor part, then scores in which only some parts are included (eg vocal score) and finally part. The definitions of the terms as used in the code are prescribed in the glossary (see comment p 12). This code also allows specification, in a note, of a library's actual holding when different, as the rule (5.5B1) requires the collation to give the actual number of parts etc issued by the publisher. This is an interesting and useful distinction, which IAML 3 does not allow for specifically. The only slight problem this poses is alteration of the note whenever a library's holdings change, but editing of any catalogue in a busy library is a larger problem of which the change of instrumentation would seem a very small part.

It should also be noted that AACR 2 requires the physical nature of the score to be indicated for vocal and chorus scores in the uniform title (rule 25.31B3). This means that this information is supplied twice at least; it could also be a part of the title or edition statement. There does not seem to be any harm in this, as long as it is supplied consistently for all kinds of score, including vocal and chorus scores, in one place. This is done most satisfactorily in the collation in these rules.

The draft ISBD (PM) has somewhat fuller rules again, which appear to be somewhat complex but in fact cover the cases which are dealt with in AACR (2) in the general rules or those for books (1.5 and 2.5.). They must obviously be included in the ISBD (PM) all in the same section. The ISBD (PM) also very usefully indicates the kind of information to be given in the note area in relation to a particular item in the collation. This, together with rules on unnumbered pages, leaves as part of a larger sequence, and complicated paginations in works in several volumes, does create a certain impression of confusion. The end result might leave a user a little daunted:

. – 1 score (2 vol. : x, 210 p; v, 310 p.)

Is such detail really necessary for music? Such information can be given using AACR 2, as rule 5.5B3 in the music section instructs the cataloguer to refer to the rules under 2.5B for expression of pagination. These relate to books, pamphlets and printed sheets and contain very detailed rules which produce similar collations to the one cited above from ISBD (PM). However, it is perfectly possible to catalogue music using the rules under 5.5B, and probably most music libraries will be content with the extent of description prescribed there. For those requiring the fullest description, either the rules for books in AACR 2 or the ISBD (PM) are available. Both of them allow for the presence of other items such as cassettes to be indicated in the collation. AACR 2 (rule 5.5E1) gives:

1 score (35 p) : ill + 4 parts; 28 cm. + 1 booklet.

Series

IAML 3 gives two categories. The first includes the names of the publisher and is defined consequently as a publisher's series eg Hawkes pocket scores. On the other hand, 'subject' series do not usually include the name of the publisher, but represent music of a certain type, era etc eg Musica Britannica. There is possibly no need to specify the first type in the series note, especially when the publisher's name appears in the imprint and the designation 'miniature score' in the collation. However, in such cases it is probably quicker to include the information than to debate the point. For the reader familiar with the series in question it gives a very clear idea of the physical format. Hence the close relation of the series note to the collation.

There is really no particular problem with this area. AACR 2 and the draft ISBD (PM) require parallel series titles to be indicated in the same way as is the practice with other such titles, and the inclusion of the ISSN (International standard serial number) when one is available. IAML 3 suggests that publisher's numbers may be treated like a series. These are not to be confused with plate numbers and usually appear on the title page. Some publishers appear to use the same number both as plate and as publisher number, eg Universal Edition's edition of Beethoven's variations on folksongs opp 105, 107 has the number UT 50017 on the cover, the title page and each page of music in the place for a plate number. This surely is a plate number irrespective of its appearance elsewhere.

Notes

Care must be taken with the notes on two counts. Firstly, it is important not to include in this area anything which really ought to be included in the main areas. Secondly, notes should be kept as brief as possible as to both their number and their actual expression. When it is necessary to include a number of notes, it is essential to keep their sequence in the same order as that of the areas forming the main body of the entry, eg notes on the imprint precede those on the collation.

Probably the two most important items to be included in the notes are the medium of performance and the duration of the work. The latter can only be an approximation, of course, but it is included in some scores and can then be easily noted. The codes allow for its use only when it is thus found. Otherwise the BBC's catalogues of its music library (*Chamber music*, 1965; *Piano and organ*, 1965; *Song*, 1966; *Choral and opera*, 1967; *Orchestral*, to be published) contain timings for many works, but by no means all. The *IAML (UK) Union Catalogue of orchestral scores and parts* (to be published in 1979) similarly gives timings for many entries, while David Daniels in his *Orchestral music* (Metuchen, N J Scarecrow Press, 1972) is more complete in his coverage of times. Details of other items giving orchestral timings can be found by reference to Vincent Duckles's *Music reference and research materials*. (3rd ed. Collier MacMillan, 1974).

Medium of performance is catered for in both codes and the ISBD (PM). None of them, unfortunately, provides a formula for expressing the instrumentation in the case of works for orchestra. It was hoped by many that AACR 2 might do this, at least in an appendix. It is an essential piece of information and various formulae exist, none of which take up too much room and can be easily included as a note. The simplest formula is set out as follows:

2222 - 4231 - timp. - str.

which means two flutes, two oboes, two clarinets, two bassoons, four horns, two trumpets, three trombones and one tuba. Timp = timpani and Str = strings, the number of players not being specified. It is of course possible to specify the different kinds of percussion and the number of string players. When the latter is done, it should be in the order violins I, violins II, violas, cellos, bass eg:

10,8642

If any of the instruments is not used it is represented by 0:

2202 - 2000 - Str.

Additional instruments can be shown in abbreviated form after the equivalent normal pitch instrument, when it is easily so related, or at the end:

2 + pic, 2 2 + a.sax, 2 etc.

means two flutes, piccolo, two oboes, two clarinets, alto saxophone, two bassoons.

2222 - 4231 - Timp - Str - Hpsc.

adds harpsichord to the original example. When a player doubles, the additional instrument can be added in curves:

2 (t. sax)

means two clarinet players, one of whom doubles on tenor saxophone. Voices can be shown after the instruments, when appropriate. Capital letters can be used for them.

S (soprano) A (alto) T (tenor), Bar (baritone) B (bass)

This of course only caters for fairly simple scores and reflects the suggestions for publishers to give such information which is prescribed in BS 4754 (British Standards Institute, 1971. Revised edition in preparation). For full professional orchestras, dance bands, jazz orchestras, brass bands etc much more complicated detail is required. This is specified from the forthcoming BBC's Catalogue of the orchestral library and is set out in appendix 2 together with the specification used for IAML (UK)'s Union Catalogue.

Whichever formula is used, as it is in the notes area it should express the holdings of the library. Thus the collation will read:

1 score (50 p) + 24 parts

and the note:

Library has 2202 - 2100 - Str

In the case of public libraries supplying amateur orchestras, they may well provide a standard number of string parts (54321 say) which will be made known to orchestras before they borrow.

The detail of the number of players (hands) for the piano can cause problems. AACR 2 gives only one example (For piano 4 hands). Many might feel 'Piano duet' was more generally understood. However, a standard numerical formula might work best. Thus:

Piano
Piano 1 hand
Piano 3 hands
Piano 4 hands
Piano 6 hands
2 Pianos 4 hands
etc

as against:

Piano
Piano 1 hand
Piano duet
2 Pianos (4 hands)
2 Pianos (8 hands)
3 Pianos (6 hands)
etc.

AACR 2 provides a similar formula in its rules for uniform titles (rule 25.29D2). Here, in order to aid alphabetical filing, the number of instruments appears after 'piano':

piano
piano, 4 hands
pianos (2)

pianos (2), 8 hands

etc.

It seems a bit like counting legs of sheep as opposed to sheep, but it is necessary for a library to have a standard formula rather than confuse the two, resulting in one note saying 'piano duet' and another '1 piano 4 hands'.

Contents notes are another important group. These should be given in paragraph form. AACR 2 requires very careful detail including, to judge from its example from Schütz's works, parallel titles. The ISBD (PM) merely comments that contents should be given. IAML 3 does not mention them, while IAML 2 has a section on contents, but not on notes. It says that the kind of library for which the code is intended may not have time to make such notes, but suggests that it would be useful to list the composers whose works are included in a composite volume, if nothing else is done. The AACR 2 rule gives the layout:

Contents: v.1. Nos 1-36 – v.2. Nos 37-66 – v.3. Nos 67-96 – v.4. Nos 97-121 – v.5. Nos 122-139 – v.6. Nos 140-153.

for Bartók's *Mikrokosmos.*

AACR 2 requires the plate or publisher's number to be given here, the latter only if the former is not available. Comment on this point has already been made in the section on imprint.

Standard number

Both AACR 2 and the draft ISBD (PM) require this to be given when available. ISBD (PM) substitutes the plate or publisher's number when the ISBN is not available. As has been stated above (p 68), the ISBN system is not used to any extent by music publishers as yet. A check in scores published in 1978 by Faber Music and the Oxford University Press, both of whom are also book publishers and use ISBN's in their books, revealed that neither apparently uses ISBN's in its music. (However, for an example of an OUP music item using an ISBN see p 131.) It is such a useful identification that it is to be hoped this practice will soon spread to music publishing.

Examples

Some examples of full entries following AACR 2 are given in appendix 1. These demonstrate the use of the punctuation system, which in AACR 2 is as prescribed by the ISBD's.

Manuscripts

AACR 2 has a separate section for the description of manuscripts (Chapter 4), but no special rules for music manuscripts. IAML 4 naturally has detailed rules for this kind of material. The amount of information to be given will vary considerably according to the purpose of the catalogue, the size of the collection and the nature of the material, particularly the period from which it comes, more detail generally being required for manuscripts dating from earlier periods than for those from the nineteenth century or later.

IAML 4 divides the description into two levels–short and detailed. The short form is to be given first immediately following the title (or incipit in the case of single works) and covers the following:

a. *Material* An indication for pre 1600 manuscripts of the material on which the music is written.

b. *Presentation* ie the method by which the music is organized. This is done by using such terms as choir book, tablature etc for older music, and score, parts etc for more recent examples.

c. *Collation* –the number of folios ie leaves.

d. *Format* size, expressed in centimetres, height x width.

e. *Authenticity, provenance, notation* If the provenance cannot be established, the phrase 'provenance unknown' is to be used. Otherwise details of origin (eg 'Autgr' if certainly autograph) provenance, and notation (eg Byzantine neumes) are to be given.

f. *Date of origin*

The detailed description amplifies these aspects in the same order; the amount of amplification is left to individual cataloguers. For example, under *Format* the measurements of individual leaves can be recorded if these vary in size. It would, in this case, be necessary to add 'average size' to the measurements given in the short description. Additionally, the detailed description includes information about the binding and illustrations, and suggests adding any extra information which may be useful. Reference can also be made to published detailed accounts of a manuscript if they are available.

The manuscript section in AACR 2 has rules the application of which would produce descriptions lacking the detail of those suggested in the short descriptions specified in IAML 4. For music manuscripts, IAML 4 would seem to give much better guidance. However, AACR 2 has rules for such items as correspondence, lectures and legal documents, all of which music libraries could well have in their care when these relate to composers, performers etc.

Microforms

This term includes a variety of forms such as microfilm, microfiche etc. They are important materials in many music libraries, particularly research libraries. It is now possible for such libraries to have microform copies of autograph manuscripts held in other collections. Such provision of copies saves musicologists much time, though they may regret the loss of an excuse to visit foreign countries so frequently.

AACR 2 has a section (chapter 11) devoted to their description. The general material designator for them is *microforms*. The rules provide guidance for specifying among other items the imprint of the microform, the number of cassettes or reels depending on the nature of the form, the width of a microfilm in millimetres etc. The title used for the title proper area will depend on the nature of the microform. If it is a microfilm of an autograph manuscript, then the title will be that of the original manuscript. If on the other hand it is a collection of material specially brought together in microform, then the title proper will be that assigned to the collection by the publisher.

AACR 2 requires the imprint, collation etc to be that of the microfrom in hand, but allows details of the original to be given in a note if this is necessary. This would enable details of an autograph manuscript to be given as specified in the IAML 4 rules for these materials, but it is obviously essential that readers know primarily the physical nature of the material they are going to handle in the library. In particular it is necessary to distinguish between published microforms and those supplied by another library on demand. This can usually be done in the imprint or in a note. Some examples of the practice at the Pendlebury Music Library, Cambridge, are provided in appendix 4.

Sound recordings

This term now covers a wide range of materials from cylinders, on which the early recordings were made, to cassettes, which have now achieved almost universally a level of reproduction equal to that of discs and on occasion surpassing it. The method of recording has changed over the last century even more frequently than has the sound carrying device. The humorous cartoons drawn by Caruso show clearly the frustrations of early recording sessions, when the artists had to gather around a device rather like a large horn and sing or play into that, the resulting waves of sound being cut straight into the recording cylinder or disc. Now (March 1979) comes the first issue of a recording where the sound has been transferred into numbers on a computer and then back into sound again, with the promise that shortly the stylus will be replaced by the laser. The computer can apparently be programmed to receive only the desired sounds and therefore, in reproducing early recordings, all the dross can be eliminated. Looking back at the history of the recording industry, there seems an inevitability about the sequence of events which has brought two of the most successful scientific developments of the twentieth century together to produce sound of a quality surpassing that heard naturally in the concert hall.

It is not possible, nor would it be appropriate, to examine here the ethics of an industry which can control a sung or played sequence of notes to the extent that it can be made very simply into a new, seemingly more beautiful, sound, so that the artist in the concert hall is in competition with a quality of performance which can never be achieved by unaided human agency. However, it is important for librarians to be aware of all the changes which occur in so important an industry, and particularly how these can affect the products which have now become a recognized part of the library service.

The development of libraries of recorded sound has generally followed very slowly behind the changes in the industry. In the United States, recordings were provided by libraries before the second world war, but in the United Kingdom, it was not until the late 1940's that records began to be made available in libraries. At each stage of industrial development there has been at least a token resistance by librarians to change. This is not unnatural and they should not be chastised for it. It is most frustrating to have spent funds on (say) mono long playing records, and then to have them replaced almost overnight by stereo recordings, which are followed almost immediately by quadraphonic sound and in physical form by reel to reel tapes, cartridges and cassettes. If that were not enough, librarians have also had to face an increasing demand for a widening of services to include other styles of music besides the rather narrow western classical music which dominated record libraries until the late 1960's, certainly in the United Kingdom. Parallel with this demand, the range of western classical music available on record has broadened astonishingly, and the companies have revitalized interest in composers whom history and the processes of human memory had relegated to limbo.

Cataloguers of recorded sound are therefore faced with a variety of constantly changing problems, particularly when it comes to attempting to describe not only what is recorded but also the physical qualities of the sound carrier. They may have to catalogue, for example, styles of music which are outside their knowledge. It would seem that, faced with this problem, they do not always draw on the resources of knowledge about different styles of music which may be avaiable among colleagues, and it may not be untimely to remind cataloguers of the value of such hidden resources. Cataloguing codes cannot attempt to cover gaps in subject knowledge which cataloguers have, but they can provide rules to help in coping with the range of styles and with the variety of physical forms.

There have been a number of cataloguing codes for recordings. As is to be expected from comments above the Americans had examined the problems and produced codes much earlier than British librarians—in the 1940s in fact (Elmer 1957). The first code to be published in the United Kingdom was AACR 1 (1967). Fairly soon after that the *Lancet* rules were published (*Non-book materials : cataloguing rules*. Prepared by the Library Association Media Cataloguing Rules Committee. National Council for Educational Technology with the Library Association, 1973). These seem to have had a rather unhappy reception, the general impression being that they made little impact and that those librarians who did adopt them have found them rather more difficult to apply than the equivalent rules in AACR 1 which they were apparently meant to replace. It is not proposed to comment on them here, as subsequent events have rather passed them by and there is an excellent criticism of them by Dave Ferris (Ferris 1975), which, while it looks at their application to non-book materials in general, does have some comments on the difficulty of using them for cataloguing sound recordings. Similar interim codes or standards were produced in Canada (*Non-book materials : the organization of integrated collections* by Jean Riddle Weihs, Shirley Lewis and Janet MacDonald. Ottowa, Canadian Library Association, 1973) and America (*Standards for cataloguing nonprint materials*, by Alma Tillin and William J Quinby. 4th ed. Washington, AECT, 1976). Both of these and the *Lancet* rules are acknowledged as having had an influence on the comparable section in AACR 2. The ISBD (NBM) was published in 1977 and was therefore too late to affect AACR 2, although as both are based on the ISBD (G) they should be compatible. IAML 5 has not yet been published. Therefore, subsequent comment here is mainly based on AACR 2. When there is no comment on ISBD (NBM) it can be assumed there is no difference between that and AACR 2.

Label

The description of sound recordings poses a number of problems, the most important of which is the source of information. There is quite naturally a desire on the part of compilers of cataloguing rules to achieve as much consistency as possible across the rules for all materials. Therefore, the primary source for recordings is declared to be the label, although ISBD (NBM) does allow that in the case of discs and cassettes the information supplied there may often be inadequate, and that the container or accompanying booklet may provide fuller details. AACR 2 makes no such admission, although it does name them as secondary sources of information for some areas of the description.

There appears to be insufficient recognition here of the complicated situation record companies often create, partly because the labels on both cassettes and discs are very small, with the consequence that it is often difficult to put adequate information on the label. The sleeve or accompanying material contains much more detail, which is sometimes at variance with that found on the label. This is particularly true of discs pressed in a foreign country. Telefunken discs, for example, have the title on the label only in German, but the cover or container gives parallel titles in German, English and French eg:

(Label) Johann Sebastian Bach : Das Orgelwerk

(Container) Joh: Seb : Bach : Das Orgelwerk/Organ works. L'oeuvre d'orgue.

Rule 6.1D1 requires parallel titles to be given as usual, but these are not often found on the label. Is this additional information to be supplied in such circumstances? Presumably, yes. If it is, it must be supplied in square brackets (rule 6.0B2). Another example from the world of jazz:

(Label) Let me tell you. . . [followed by titles of various numbers, played by groups, mostly led by Albert Nicholas, interspersed with speech tracks. Speaker is not indicated]

(Sleeve) Let me tell you/Albert Nicholas

The sleeve makes it quite plain that this is a sequence of reminiscences by Albert Nicholas interspersed with numbers by various groups, mostly led by him, and gives details of personnel.

The risk with the sleeve and accompanying literature is that it may become detached from the disc or cassette of which it is a part. In fact, while the accompanying material is quite frequently lost, the container seems to remain fairly faithfully attached to the principal contents. In many years of buying second hand records, I have not often found discs which have the sleeve missing. When this has occurred, the basic information has nearly always been supplied on a new container. Some sort of container is an essential item of protection with a microgroove disc, and is thus a vital feature in inducing a purchase. In fact, it is true to say that the sleeve is an essential part of a disc, more than likely to stay with it. This is less true of the cassette, which by its very size does not allow for the same wealth of information, even on the container, as is frequently provided with a disc.

This may seem a small point, but if AACR 2 insists, as it rightly does, on correct cataloguing in accordance with long traditions, it means that the title and statement of responsibility area is more often than not going to derive its information other than from the primary source, and therefore that most of the detail in the title area will frequently appear in square brackets. Perhaps the most curious element in all this is that it allows accompanying textual material on the container to be used as a secondary source of information in all other areas of the description except that of the title and statement of responsibility. If there are two or more chief sources of information, eg two labels on a disc, it allows them to be treated as one. Why cannot the label and the container be treated in the same way? Surely this is how the record industry treats them? AACR 2, and to a slightly lesser extent ISBD (NBM), has created an unnecessary problem here.

It could of course be argued that in the case of 78 rpm discs the sleeve usually gave no information about the recording, so that AACR 2's rules fit all cases, but this would be equally true of a rule treating label, container and accompanying literature as a single chief source. Part of the difficulty here as in other situations is that the examples chosen tend to fit the rules. Unfortunate, indeed is the cataloguer who has to cope with examples which do not do so! There are likely to be many such examples and they will be treated in different ways, producing the very inconsistencies it was hoped to avoid.

Performers

AACR 2 has provided a rule for the statement of responsibility (6.1F1) which with regard to its treatment of performers is much better than the parallel rule (1.5.1) in ISBD (NBM). The latter requires the names of performers to be included in the statement of responsibility area even when their contribution is limited to performance, whereas in such circumstances with classical music AACR 2 relegates them to the notes area in accordance with previous practice. At the very least they ought to be in a clearly separated and secondary part of the statement of responsibility. With popular, jazz or rock artists AACR 2 recognizes a different situation, and they are to be included in the statement of responsibility area.

However, AACR 2 does not appear to have covered the many classical recordings on which an artist performs a number of items by different composers. The title on the recording may be either in the form:

Janet Baker sings English songs

or:

English songs. Janet Baker.

Presumably the title proper in the first case is *Janet Baker sings English songs*. In the second, the performer's name is relegated by the code to a note. However, in the section on the formulation of headings, rule 21.23C provides for the entry of such recordings under the name of the artist. This recognizes the significance of the artist's rôle in these circumstances, and the total entry therefore makes very good sense. For further comment on rule 21.23C see p 99.

Multiple works on a recording

Neither AACR 2 nor ISBD (NBM) seem to have catered for the many boxed sets which are issued nowadays containing a large number of items by an equally large number of composers, eg the Qualiton recording *Music life in old Hungary* contains thirty nine items. Both codes require contents lists to be given as a part of the notes area, but unfortunately each gives examples with a very limited number of works to be itemised. Again it is a failure to cater adequately for a complex situation and to provide satisfactory examples. The Qualiton set poses further problems as there is a large number of artists and groups involved. AACR 2 has an example in which there are different performers for each work included. They are cited in curves after each title in the contents note. Is this to be done for thirty nine items? Obviously each library will have its own rules for such a case. A research library such as the British Institute of Recorded Sound will probably want analytical entries for each work as well as full description, whereas a public library or a recreational library in an academic institution will probably content itself with a brief note that the set contains thirty nine items. While it is important to realize that a code cannot cater for every case in its rules, its examples ought surely to show how difficult examples are to be handled under the rules provided.

Use of trade name

It has been standard practice in cataloguing discs to use the trade or brand name as equivalent to publisher in the imprint area eg Das alte Werk is preferred to Telefunken, Turnabout to Decca. AACR 2 continues this practice, although rule 6.4D3 states:

> If, however, a trade name appears to be the name of a series rather than of a publishing subdivision, record it as a series. In case of doubt treat the name as a series.

This is reasonable, except that it is probable that under this rule more such trade names will be treated as series. They will certainly be treated differently by various cataloguers eg Das alte Werk and Archive are examples which could easily be doubtful cases. Classics for pleasure is fairly clearly a subdivision of EMI, but is Concert classics a subdivision or a series? At one time both would have been entered in the imprint.

ISBD (NBM) is firmly against the use of such labels in the imprint. They are to be included as a series, if obviously one, or in the standard number area.

Physical description

This has become rather fuller than was the practice in the past. A full collation following AACR 2 would read:

1 sound disc (45 min.) : 33⅓ rpm, stereo; 12 in.

1 sound cassette (50 min.) : 3¾ ips, stereo.

For sound cassettes the dimensions do not have to be given if they are the standard size 3⅞ x 2½ in). ISBD (NBM)'s collation for the same information would be the same except that the measurement of size is in centimetres. It is perhaps a little perverse of AACR 2 to give the size in inches only, when certainly the United Kingdom is changing to the metric system.

ISBD (NBM) does not allow for the timing of individual works to be given, which is a disadvantage. AACR 2 allows a separately titled part of a sound recording to be described separately if the recording lacks a collective title (rule 6.1G4). In such cases the timing of each title is given after an indication of the fractional extent of each piece in the form:

On sides 2 and 3 of 4 sound discs (55 mins)

On 1 track of 1 sound cassette (25 mins)

There is unfortunately no indication of how to express the fraction of a side (eg a half side) which many works occupy. This used to be shown in the form (AACR 1 rule 252.D.1):

½s. 12 in. 33⅓ rpm.

The procedure suggested in the first edition of this work for libraries whose stock consists entirely of recordings in one physical form can still be followed, even when cassettes as well as discs are part of the stock: ie if all the discs are 12 in long playing records and there are no cassettes, the collation need only express how many channels:

Stereo

If cassettes are added, then the collation can similarly say either:

1 sound disc mono
or
1 sound cassette mono
etc.

Standard numbers

No system of international standard numbers exists as yet for sound recordings. ISBD (NBM) suggests including the manufacturer's list number (eg HMV ALP 1234, Decca SXL 1234 etc) in this area. AACR 2 requires this information to be given in the notes area. It always used to be given immediately after the name of the label in the imprint (AACR 1 rule 252 C1). There was an advantage in this, as those persons who listen extensively to records can as easily identify a recording and its particular quality by the list number as by the label or trade name. It also gave some indication to an expert of the date, when this was uncertain. This latter aspect is less important now that record companies are giving the copyright date, since the Universal Copyright Convention came into force in 1955, but nevertheless there is much to be said for retaining the link between label and list number. If the latter has to be moved, the new area accorded it by ISBD (NBM) seems more logical.

Conclusion

The description of music whether in manuscript, print or recorded sound needs to be done with care. Some areas still have their confusions, even with all the careful work that has gone into AACR 2 and the ISBDs. Nevertheless, in most libraries a cataloguer with knowledge of music should not find it too difficult to arrive at a description satisfactory for most users. Areas where there are difficulties have been touched on in this chapter. Two broad categories of material remain relatively uncovered by codes and standards. These are early recordings and ethnomusicological materials. Help in cataloguing the former can be gained by reference to the many excellent published discographies which exist (Foreman 1973 & 1974). For the latter much remains to be done. Part of the problem is that ethnomusicologists seem themselves to be uncertain about their subject (Woakes 1978). A basis for developing a code of practice for describing their materials exist in the ISBDs, and it is possible that research may be undertaken in the United States into the needs of ethnomusicologists and how they can be satisfied by music libraries. (Kaufmann 1977 p 13).

Examples

See appendix 1 for some examples of the application of AACR 2 to particular cases, including the Britten work cited above (p 66) as an example of standard practice before the introduction of ISBDs. In particular the examples in the appendix demonstrate the application of the punctuation practice, which is so important an element in organizing the description, especially in machine readable form. Examples for IAML 3 are not given, as there are several in Appendix 1 of that publication.

CHAPTER FOUR

HEADINGS

AS AN introduction to this chapter it is difficult to find better words than those which begin the same section in AACR 2 (20.1 on p 277):

> When a standard description for an item has been established according to the rules in Part 1, headings and/or uniform titles are normally added to that description to create catalogue entries. The only exception is when an entry is made under title proper, in which case entry is made under the first words of the description.

In this book uniform titles have been examined first, because they are regarded by most cataloguers of music as having a central key rôle in the organization of music entries in a catalogue. They link the chosen heading to the description and sometimes add further information to that found in the latter.

As long as the compilers of cataloguing codes continue the concept of main or principal entry, cataloguers will have to continue to make a decision as to which is the most likely sought term under which to place the fullest description of an item, so that users of the catalogue will find it quickly. In the vast majority of cases in dealing with western classical music, both in written and recorded form, there is no problem. The most suitable heading is the form of name generally recognized for a composer. There is sometimes the problem of joint authorship where two or more persons collaborate to create a work, but such co-operation is not frequently found in classical music. Thus for the compositions of Hugo Wolf most persons will go straight to the form of heading adopted for that composer's name. The only alternatives with such a composer are the titles or first lines of the poems set by him. (For the musical setting, the poet's or librettist's name is surely not a serious contender.) With a composer like Arcangelo Corelli, who wrote apparently only within the framework of instrumental musical forms, the use of title is much less likely.

The problem is less easily solved with other styles of music (and, of course, with record albums containing works by several classical composers). Folk music, for example, can be sought equally under the title of a song and the name of a performer, and the collocative function of catalogues may best be served by using the title as main entry in this case. Jazz records quite often have one artist named as the principal performer, but there are many examples, like the album entitled *Duke Ellington & John Coltrane*, when the choice is less clear. For ethnomusicological recordings the main entry could be under either a geographical area, a social custom or a musical instrument, rather than under a personal name.

With the rapidly growing use of computers for the compilation of catalogues, the concepts of main and added entries become less and less important. Once the basic description has been fed into the computer, the machine can be instructed to reproduce that unit of description under as many headings as are necessary and are supplied to it. In fact even this is not a new concept. Many libraries which have facilities for reproducing entries cheaply once the basic description has been created, have for a long time used their own basic unit card and reproduced as many copies of these as are necessary for the different headings an item may require. Alternatively, the purchase of the required number of BNB or LC cards is another way of providing the basic unit of description, over which, in all these cases, the appropriate headings are typed.

All these practices reduce the necessity for the consideration of the question in relation to an item—'What is the most likely sought heading under which it should be placed?'—as the full information is found under all the headings thought to be likely sought terms. Care needs to be taken, of course, in deciding what constitutes the unit of description over which the headings are to be placed, as such decisions will affect the filing. If the unit of description includes the main entry heading, as it does for example when BNB cards are used, then under an added entry heading it will file logically in a different place from that under which it would file if the basic description is seen as starting with the uniform title or with the title proper. Thus:

Beethoven, Ludwig van
    [Concerto piano . . .]
    Piano concerto

could file under an added entry heading for editor's name at letter B C or P. Proper rules for filing are crucial in this situation in order to maintain consistency. See the *ALA rules for filing catalog cards* (2nd ed Chicago, ALA, 1968) for a full discussion of this problem.

The quotation from AACR 2 at the beginning of this chapter makes it plain that the descriptive unit as far as AACR 2 is concerned is to begin at the title proper. Unfortunately, there appears to be no actual example showing how an added entry heading should be set out in relation to the descriptive unit. This may have been done deliberately in order to allow libraries to organize the filing of their entries in the way that suits them best.

Many of the general rules on choice of access points in AACR 2 (Chapter 21) affect decisions about musical works and recordings. When cataloguing music, reference to them will need to be made constantly, and indeed some of them quote musical examples. Musical works come in the section 21.18 to 21.22 and sound recordings under 21.23. Once the choice of access has been made, the form of name appropriate for the choice has to be decided. For this, chapters 22 to 24 are the guides. It is not proposed to deal with these chapters here as there are no special problems for music. The specific problems occur in deciding the access point.

However, there is one point to make in relation to deciding the form of name. That relates to rule 22.1A:

> Choose, as the basis of the heading for a person, the name by which he or she is commonly known.

Surely the name by which Beethoven is known is 'Beethoven' not 'Ludwig van Beethoven'. There is a time factor here in a large catalogue. A great deal of time could be saved by not using 'Wolfgang Amadeus' to identify *the* Mozart. Everybody knows which is meant. Entries under Mozart's son and father would appear in the form

Mozart, Franz Xavier
Mozart, Leopold

thus bringing *the* Mozart's entries to the front of the sequence. The same method could be used for the far more numerous Bach family. Again everybody knows which is *the* Bach. A small point, but the practice of such a system could save a lot of time in typing. AACR 2 has nevertheless moved a long way from the original American position which required entries like:

Mŏzart, Johann Chrysostom Wolfgang Amadeus, 1756-1791

An additional typist must have been needed!

Choice of access–Music

The basic rules in AACR 2, which are equally applicable to music, require entry under the personal author (rules 21.1A2 and 21.4A).

This will cover most classical music satsifactorily, and in rule 21.1A1 composers of music are defined as authors of the works they create. The IAML codes all agree with this as a basic rule for personal authorship.

Corporate authorship is unlikely to affect published classical music. The rule in AACR 2 (21.1B2) divides corporate authors into various categories, of which e) is relevant to recorded music as it covers 'sound recordings, films and video-recordings which result from the collective activity of a performing group' when that activity 'goes beyond that of mere performance, execution etc'. This is a curious phrase which seems to imply that performance is relatively unimportant. 'Mere' is not necessary; also the rule should surely be widened to cover the publication of such items in print form. IAML 3 has a rule (1.41) for corporate authorship which requires entry of a work under the name of a corporate body which is clearly responsible for the content. It quotes an example which would not apparently fit any of the five categories in AACR 2:

U.S. Army language school . . .
Japanese songs

Presumably AACR 2 requires this to be entered under title (rule 21.1C). The wording of the rule for corporate authorship in AACR 2 is less than precise as it omits the crucial words which appear in IAML 3's rule: *clearly responsible for the content.*

Liturgical works are of course to be entered under the heading for the church or other religious organization when the music is an officially prescribed part of the liturgy (AACR 2: rule 21.22. IAML 3: 1.42). The IAML 3 rule extends it to cover hymnals and similar publications, when these are officially prescribed. AACR 2 has a separate rule (21.39A3) for such items as hymnals, programmes of religious services etc, with the instruction to enter in accordance with the general rules 21.1–21.7. Each case has to be treated, therefore, according to those different rules. *The book of Common prayer* appears as an example under rule 21.4B with the instruction to enter under the heading for the church. Thus a tune book for *The school hymn book of the Methodist Church* would go under the heading for the church, while *Songs of praise with music* would be entered under Vaughan Williams with added entries under Martin Shaw as joint composer/ editor of the music and Percy Dearmer as editor of the text (rule 21.6B2).

Works of unknown authorship are entered under the title. AACR 2 (rule 21.1C) extends title entry to cover works issued by those corporate bodies which do not fall into one of its five categories. It is difficult to fit hymn books into one of these categories, but, as has been shown, they can, as official publications, be entered under the heading for a church. The IAML 3 rule (1.2) covers changes of title, requiring entry under the original unless one of the later titles is better known or more frequently used. The index to AACR 2 does not reveal a similar rule. However, by analogy with its rule for uniform title, entry will be under the original title without exception.

Works of shared responsibility

Both codes have basically the same rules, ie that if one composer is clearly the principal author by disposition of the title page, entry is to be under that composer's name, otherwise under the one first named on the title page. This applies up to three composers. If there are more than three, IAML 3 requires entry under title, as does AACR 2 unless one, two or three is/are clearly the principal composer(s). (IAML 3: rules 1.121 and 1.122. AACR 2: rules under 21.6.) This situation of shared responsibility does not occur that frequently in classical music, but is more common in light music, particularly with musical comedies and shows. There are no particular problems in applying the rules.

Collections and works produced under editorial direction

AACR 2 (rules under 21.7) directs that these are entered under title. IAML 3 requires entry under editor if named on the title page (rule 1.52). Neither rule applies, of course, to a collected edition of an individual composer, but to such collections of works by many composers as:

Musica Britannica
Denkmäler deutscher Tonkunst
Le pupitre

The AACR 2 rule places such a collection under a more suitable heading, which will be consistent with other entries for similar works, while the IAML 3 rule varies the kind of entry according to the appearance or not of the editor's name on the title page.

Works of mixed responsibility:
Arrangements, adaptations etc

The IAML codes recognize that it is often difficult to distinguish the kind of relationships here and how much reorganization of the original work has occurred. This can be quite a problem if the cataloguer does not have a knowledge of music. IAML 1 has a technical analysis of the problem which requires a knowledge of harmony etc to apply (pp 36-38). IAML 2 (p 18) gives a rule of thumb which can be applied by cataloguers without a knowledge of music:

a) if the title includes "adaptation", "arrangement", "reduction", "transcription", the author chosen is the author of the original work.
b) if the title includes "fantasy...", "pot-pourri on...", "variations on..." heading chosen is the name of the arranger...

IAML 3 establishes two categories, ie arrangements and adaptations. Arrangements are entered under the original composer, adaptations under the composers of the adaptations. In case of doubt, entry is under the original composer. 'Arrangements' cover editions where, for example, a work for solo instrument and orchestra has been arranged for solo instrument and piano eg:

Mozart's violin concerto no 1
arranged for violin or viola and piano

or where the original key has been transposed. The essential point is that the work is recognizably the same as the original as far as harmony, structure etc is concerned. In an adaptation, this technical detail has been altered eg:

Beethoven's variations on "God save the king".

AACR 1 seemed to require a knowledge of harmony for its rules to be applied (rules 231-2). This has been simplified by AACR 2, which now has two rules (21.18B and C) almost identical to those in IAML 3 with some excellent examples.

Musical works with words

AACR 2 (rule 21.19A) requires entry under the composer, while IAML 3 has no specific rule, but the example of the work by Gagnebin under rule 1.111 makes it clear that entry is under the composer. Both codes require ballad operas, pasticcios etc to be entered under title (AACR 2: rule 21.19B1. IAML 3: rule 1.35).

Related works:

AACR 2 has a general rule which directs that entry should be made under the heading for the related work, not that for the original work (rule 21.28B). Included by the code in this category are libretti, cadenzas and incidental music to dramatic works. For the last there would be no difficulty in a music library. Grieg's *Peer Gynt* clearly is entered under Grieg, not under Ibsen.

Libretti

This is another area of uncertainty. Really the only solution is triple entry under composer, librettist and title. The codes vary:

IAML 1 : Title
IAML 2 : Librettist or title
IAML 3 : Composer if named in text, otherwise title
AACR 2 : Librettist
AACR 2 : Composer (alternative rule)

Cadenzas

A distinction is drawn in all codes except IAML 1 between separately published cadenzas and those published with the original work. The former go under the composer of the cadenzas, the latter (apparently by inference in using AACR 2 and IAML 2) under the composer of the original work. In both cases added entries are made under the other composer. The wording of the AACR 2 rule (21.28A) is not actually clear:

> ... apply this rule to separately catalogued works

Presumably this means separately published works. The treatment of cadenzas published with the original work is not clear. IAML 2 (p 19) also makes no mention of cadenzas published with the original, but separately published ones go under their composer. IAML 3 (rule 1.34) is the only code to differentiate clearly between the two publication states. IAML 1 (p 36) appears to be quite emphatic that they all go under the original composer. Once again this is a quite clear case for abandoning the idea of a single main entry, and having double entry under both composers in both situations.

Sound recordings

Only AACR 2 has rules for these. The special rules appear on pages 314-5.

Single works

There is apparently no problem here. They are entered under the heading appropriate to the work. In spite of this rather cautious wording, instead of using the words 'under the author or composer', all the examples given are entered under the author or composer. Under 21.4A, however, an example used to demonstrate the principle enunciated in that rule ('enter a work, a collection of works, or selections from a work or works by one personal author under the heading for that person') is the recording *The indispensable Earl Hines* with the instruction to 'enter under heading for Hines'. In the recordings section, rule 21.23C covers the situation:

> Enter a sound recording containing works by different persons under the heading for the person or body represented as principal performer.

This is very reasonable except that, as suggested in chapter one (p 29), there are situations when only one work is recorded and the interest lies principally in the performer rather than the composer. It is analogous to the question of arrangement/adaptation with printed music. In such recordings the original music has been transformed and the performance is best thought of as a set of variations on the original. Thus the Miles Davis recording of *Porgy and Bess* (CBS 62108) is referred to as *Miles Davis's Porgy and Bess*, not Gershwin's. The front of the cover does not even mention George Gershwin. There seems a clear case here for treating such jazz performances under the heading for the performer, with added entry under the composer and the arranger (Gil Evans, in this case) if named.

Rule 21.23C needs interpretation, which should surely have been given in the rule itself, in its application to classical recordings. As it stands it implies quite clearly that the recording of Prokofiev's *Quintet* op 39 and Shostakovich's *Quintet* op 57 by the Melos Ensemble (L'Oiseau-Lyre, SOL 267) is to be entered under the heading appropriate to the performers. This would be totally contrary to standard practice in libraries for recordings containing up to three works. However, in the rules for description, rule 6.1G4 says:

> If desired, make a separate description for each separately titled work on a sound recording...

and rule 6.7B21

> If the description is of a separately titled part of a sound recording lacking a collective title, make a note beginning *With*: and listing the other separately titled parts of the item...

These two rules from the description area allow this treatment only when the recording lacks a collective title. Surely this is irrelevant with up to three works? One other point the rule about 'With' notes (6.7B21) does not make clear is that, in order to link works in this way, the 'With' note must give the title of the work referred to in its uniform title form, if these titles are used and the user is to be directed to the proper place in the catalogue *in all cases*, not just when an item lacks a title.

When there are works by different persons recorded by more than three principal performers, entry is under title (21.23D). If there is no collective title, entry is to be under the heading appropriate to the first work or contribution named in the chief source of information (21.7C). Again for classical works entry would be preferable under each work up to three with linking 'With' notes.

Recordings of non-western music

Reference has already been made (p 29) to Judith Kaufman's most useful contribution to the study of this complex area (Kaufman 1977). She further points out that titles and names of performers and composers are frequently unknown. Entry is therefore under subject headings, for which she analyzes the headings used by LC in the period 1973-76, showing how entries for the music of a single cultural group are scattered throughout the catalogue. It is a short but very valuable investigation which needs much wider circulation than it has so far received, particularly in the United Kingdom. It is probable that the questionnaire which she circulated to thirty three American libraries associated with courses in ethnomusicology would be even more revealing than it was in America if it were to be circulated to the equivalent British libraries. Of the twenty six American libraries replying, no two worked the same system. IAML's Cataloguing Commission is beginning to discuss the problem and may produce a thesaurus of terms.

Transliteration (romanization)

This problem, which affects all styles of music, was touched on in chapter one (see p 21). The main concern is consistency. Romanization is important here more than in any other part of an entry, as the heading determines the primary filing term. Chaikovskiĭ, while correct, would lose him for most people. However, his name is the major change for most catalogues. It might help posterity to make the change now. At least one commercial firm (May & May) has done it without fuss.

CHAPTER FIVE

SUBJECT CATALOGUING

THIS ASPECT of cataloguing is, like all the topics discussed in the previous chapters, a matter of endless debate among librarians. There are a number of excellent books on the subject, and it is not proposed to do more here than draw the reader's attention to a number of different systems which have or could have application to music. Two books are quite outstanding (Coates 1960 & Foskett 1977) and repay careful study. Anyone requiring full information on all aspects of the subject approach to knowledge will find them a mine of information. Eric Coates's is probably the finest mind working on the problems of organizing knowledge, and his book has already achieved the status of a classic. A C Foskett's book is much more recent and much wider in scope, mainly because so many systems have developed since Coates wrote his book. Foskett writes very clearly and explains complicated systems such as PRECIS (PREserved Context Indexing System) in terms that the layman can understand, which is not always true of official pronouncements. The references and bibliography are of course very much more up to date in Foskett's book and are an invaluable feature.

The subject approach in cataloguing attempts to answer two types of question, both of them formulated by Cutter in his list of objectives:

1 Does the library have this book which is on this subject (Specific subject approach)?

2 What books does the library have on this subject and related subjects (the co-ordinating approach)?

In music catalogues a very important aspect, which is usually related to the subject approach, is the approach to music for a particular instrument and for a number of performers. This is not really a subject approach at all. Shostakovich's string quartets are not about four string players any more than Britten's *Serenade for tenor, horn and orchestra* is about the difficulty of writing for such an ensemble. Music has no subject. Nevertheless, it is usual to refer to the approach to music by terms such as strings, quartet, tenor, horn and orchestra loosely as a subject enquiry. It is in fact more accurate to call it an executant approach, as these are all examples of what Coates defines as 'executants' in BCM. Closely related, but less commonly used, is the form approach. This line of enquiry in the subject catalogue is frequently used in literature via such terms as 'poetry' and 'drama'. It is a secondary approach in music, as Coates recognized, probably more frequently used in enquiries for the literature about music than by musicians seeking music. When it is the literature about music that is sought and it is an enquiry about a form, it is a subject approach eg Arthur Hutchings book on *The Baroque concerto* (3rd ed Faber, 1973) is about the concerto as a form. The subject is the 'Baroque concerto' or the 'concerto form in the Baroque period'. When a conductor asks for the score of a Vivaldi concerto, the enquiry is for a piece of music written in concerto form. The book will illuminate the subject of concerto form, of which Vivaldi wrote many examples. The two kinds of enquiry are very different, and it may be best to follow the practice of many continental libraries and provide a separate catalogue for each category.

Continental method

IAML 2 discusses this problem, proposing that the 'subject' catalogue be kept quite separate from the composer catalogue, and that it provide entries under 'types', 'forms' and 'instruments'. There is some confusion once again over the use of the words 'form' and 'type' in English, as the examples given under 'type' seem to be forms (eg oratorio, cantata). Musicians and their associates employ terms very loosely and sometimes create thereby difficulties which really do not exist. The kind of catalogues proposed in IAML 2 are really very simple to make and to use. They must surely commend themselves for use in libraries and sections intended mainly for performers.

Two kinds of catalogue are created–for *forms* and *executants*. An example of this kind of catalogue in use would be to derive entries for a piano concerto under terms as follows:

Concerto (Form catalogue)
Piano (Executant catalogue)
Orchestra (Executant catalogue)

Thus a conductor seeking a work for his orchestra to perform would find entries for all kinds of orchestral works under the heading 'Orchestra' in the executant catalogue, including those for piano concertos. Similarly, an approach via piano in the same catalogue would reveal the works for that instrument, including piano concertos. Many librarians would hold the view that IAML 2's suggestion of a form catalogue is unnecessary for a collection of performance material. Whatever particular approaches are used, the entries under each term are arranged alphabetically by composer.

Entries can also be made under the size of the performing group, subdivided perhaps into Strings, Strings & Wind, Strings & Keyboard, Wind & Keyboard etc etc. It implies a fair proportion of staff time being spent on the compilation of such catalogues, but they certainly supply information for users in a most direct and simple way while perhaps lacking the sophistication of other more complex systems.

Classified Catalogue

When a music library is part of a larger unit, it may well have its choice of catalogue dictated for it by the kind of catalogue in use throughout the library, especially when the cataloguing process is centralized. In the United Kingdom, the choice is likely to be the classified catalogue, the advantage of which lies mainly in the systematic way in which the catalogue can be organized, especially when some technique such as chain indexing is used. Alphabetical order is not as simple as ABC, as the existence of complicated filing rules proves. The use of symbols, provided by a classification scheme, to arrange entries in a catalogue does become necessary, however, within each class number and in arranging the composer/author/title and subject indexes, but in all the latter, if they are arranged separately, the problem of alphabetization is less acute than in a dictionary catalogue, where different kinds of entries are frequently all arranged in one sequence.

The merit of the classified catalogue does depend to some extent on the classification scheme on which it is based, but presumably the latter will have been chosen for the order it produces on the shelves and if that is desirable in arranging the material, it will be equally useful in the catalogue. The classified catalogue, when used with chain indexing technique, does reveal a variety of supplementary orders in the alphabetical subject index. This is achieved with all classification schemes, but it is shown to the best advantage with a faceted scheme such as BCM, where a sample taken at random reveals the following:

Classified file:

QPE	Piano sonatas
RE	Organ sonatas
SPE	Violin & piano sonatas
WTPME	Unaccompanied horn sonatas

Subject index:

Sonatas : Horn : Solos, unaccompanied	WTPME
Sonatas : Organ	RE
Sonatas : Piano	QPE
Sonatas : Violin & piano	SPE

In this example, the classification scheme has separated the *form* sonatas because the primary facet in this scheme is *executant*, which is subdivided by the *form* facet. By using chain indexing technique, each focus in the subordinate facets can be brought together in the alphabetical arrangement to reveal other orders and thereby meet other lines of enquiry. The other elements are revealed very simply by the chain from the main class to the specific number for a particular subject:

BBC	Bach
AR	Organ
A/Y	Fugue
A/RM	Counterpoint
BBCAR/Y/RM	Bach's counterpoint in his organ fugues.

From that chain it is possible to make the following index entries simply by indexing each essential step in turn:

Counterpoint : Fugues : Organ : Bach	BBCAR/Y/RM
Fugues : Organ : Bach	BBCAR/Y
Organ : Bach	BBCAR
Bach	BBC

In indexing it is simplest to proceed from the most specific point in the chain to the broadest. At each link in the chain the element in the symbol representing the previous lower link is removed. Thus at

Fugues : organ : Bach	BBCAR/Y

the /RM for counterpoint is removed. Each of these index entries will, of course, be arranged in alphabetical order in the subject index.

By making these index entries, various other approaches to the material have been met, different from the basic one selected by the classification scheme. Thus in BCM the material is arranged by composer, but the index supplies arrangements by instrument, form and element. Presumably the majority of readers will be satsified by the composer order on the shelves, if the classification scheme has been carefully selected with the needs of most readers in mind, but the person interested in counterpoint will be guided to this book by the index, even though it is not arranged with other books on the subject at A/RM.

This method of compiling a catalogue does have advantages with music, as the subject can be broken up fairly neatly into its component facets, even when the subjects the books deal with are fairly complex. To use the catalogue the reader does not need any knowledge of chain indexing technique. It does not reveal to him immediately the presence of a book on

Bach : Organ : Fugues : Counterpoint

but if he does search in this way, as he might, then the entry under *Bach* will take him to an appropriate starting point in the classified sequence. If this sequence is adequately guided, as indeed it must be as a part of this method, then he will have no difficulty in finding the particular aspect of Bach's work he wishes to study. The simplicity of this drill can be tested quite easily by using the subject index in one of the annual volumes of the British catalogue of music. (See the section below on PRECIS for further discussion of this aspect p 111)

Chain indexing technique can be used nearly as effectively with the enumerative schemes, as this example from LC will show:

M5	–	M1459	Instrumental music
M6	–	M176	Solo
M6	–	M39	Keyboard
M20	–	M39	Piano
M23			Sonatas

Index:

Sonatas : Piano	M23
Piano solos	M20 – M39
Keyboard instruments	M6 – M39
Solos : Instrumental music	M6 – M176
Instrumental music	M

As can be seen, the method has to be adapted slightly, and care must be taken to see that each step in the chain is enumerated. In indexing, natural phrases should be used wherever appropriate:

Piano solos

rather than

Piano : Solos

although there is something to be said for following the same pattern throughout in a method such as this. Not all links need to be indexed; some librarians might decide to ignore such entries as

Solos : Instrumental music.

It is only necessary to qualify each entry term by such terms in the chain as are essential to show the precise aspect of the subject:

Sonatas : Piano

not

Sonatas : Piano : Keyboard : Solos : Instrumental music.

However, it is important to remember that qualifying terms in an index entry, however many there may be, are always arranged in reverse order to the chain sequence. Thus the chain reads

Piano
    Sonatas

therefore the index must be

Sonatas : Piano

not

Piano Sonatas.

The simplicity of the method is only fully realized if this basic rule is observed. It also reduces the number of entries which have to be made, thereby making it both an economic and a systematic method. In using the method in a general library, of course, the final qualifying term 'music' would have to be added. In a special department it can be taken for granted.

Dictionary Catalogue

This type of catalogue is most widely used in America. It has very few adherents on the Continent but quite a number in Great Britian. For its successful use it is necessary to compile the subject headings from one of the published lists, or to employ one of the mechanical methods such as chain indexing for doing this.

The dictionary catalogue is arranged in one alphabetical sequence, which includes entries for composers, authors, titles and subject, although in recent years the Americans have developed the divided dictionary catalogue, in which the different kinds of entry are arranged in separate alphabetical sequences. This fact alone is evidence of the difficulty of alphabetical arrangement. Further evidence can be obtained by comparing the LC Catalog *Music, books on music and sound recordings*, a composer catalogue with subject index, with the *BCM*. The music catalogue of Liverpool Public Libraries, which to some extent avoids many of the difficulties inherent in the dictionary catalogue by not using specific entries, is further proof of the problems to be met in this kind of catalogue when it is used in a large library. In fact it is seen at its best in a catalogue to a fairly small collection, and can possibly be recommended here in preference to the classified catalogue.

The basis of the syndetic dictionary catalogue as far as subject entries are concerned is that each item is entered under the most specific subject head that will contain it; or, to put it another way, the subject heading is coextensive with the subject of the book. The selected heading is then linked with related headings by a system of references. These references should ideally be made in all directions, but are generally only made from more general subjects to the specific subjects which they contain for reasons of economy. Sometimes references are made from co-ordinate subjects, that is, equally specific subjects:

Symphonies *See also* Sonatas

where it is felt that readers are likely to be interested in both. References are also made from synonyms which are not used as subject headings:

Folk music *See* Folk songs.

Probably the most generally used method of organizing such a subject catalogue is to base it on one of the published lists of subject headings. For a special library, the two general lists issued in America (Sears, 1972, and the LC, 1975) will not be detailed enough. Such libraries will find the *Music subject headings authorized for use in the catalogs of the music division* [of New York Public Library Reference Department] useful (Boston, Hall, 1959). A foreword to the list explains the use of the headings provided.

This is a list which has developed to its present somewhat complicated form over a long period of time in a large public library. An examination of one or two of the terms will give some indication of its structure. For convenience, references are shown in square brackets, although they are not so shown in the list.

Oboe [s.a. English horn, Shawm, etc. See Flute for headings]

Oboe – Bibl. See OBOE MUSIC – BIBL.

Oboe – Instruction

Oboe music – Bibl.

Oboe – Orchestra studies [x Orchestra – Studies]

Oboe and Bassoon [xx Bassoon and Oboe]

Oboe, Clarinet and string orchestra [xx Clarinet, Oboe and string orchestra]

Oboe, flute, trumpet and string orchestra

See FLUTE, OBOE, TRUMPET AND STRING ORCHESTRA

Oboe in trios (oboe, bassoon, piano)
See PIANO IN TRIOS (PIANO, OBOE, BASSOON)

This continues to cover all possible combinations up to

Oboe in decets

Sonata [xx Sonata da camera, Sonata da chiesa x Chamber music]
criticism or analyses of sonatas by individual composers do not take this heading.
Duplicate under instrument involved; e.g. a work on the piano sonata has subject 2 –
Piano – music

It is difficult to see why the heading 'piano sonatas' is not used here. In fact this heading is not given at all. For some unspecified reason this list uses x for *See also* references and xx for *See* references, the reverse of the generally accepted way. These two examples do reveal the problems which the cataloguer faces in compiling subject headings. Frequently, two entries have to be made if the item is to be satsifactorily entered, as in the case of instrumental forms such as piano sonatas. In addition, a very complex structure of subdivisions soon develops under one subject heading such as oboe. This is not easy to arrange alphabetically, and consequently the reader may well be confused. The Music Division of New York Public Library Reference Department is justly famous for its service, and therefore librarians using this list for their own libraries know that it is based on good experience. If they are convinced that the dictionary catalogue is the better of the two traditional forms, they will find this list a good basis on which to work.

The aim of the New York list is to try to meet all likely approaches. Therefore, as it is a dictionary catalogue, there is an entry of a composer's works under his name, while additional entries are provided by the list under instruments for the person interested in playing and under forms for the scholar. Thus for a suite for clarinet two headings are provided:

Suites (Clarinet)

Clarinet music.

Such detailed treatment bulks the catalogue and some librarians may prefer to use the simpler list which can be built up from the music catalogue published by Liverpool Public Libraries. Entries are made under the composer and the instrument, which is subdivided into technique, solo, instrument and piano, duos etc. An exception is made for symphonies, but in the case of a composer like Haydn the reader is simply referred to the entry under the composer. The complicated treatment for ensembles in the New York list can be contrasted with the method used at Liverpool where such scores are brought together under 'Chamber music', sub-arranged by size and then by instruments. The New York list has the advantage of bringing everything relating to one instrument together under its name. In the Liverpool catalogue, entries under forms are limited to books about the particular form. References are very restricted, but the catalogue is easy to use and does add point to the criticism that references often confuse rather than help the reader.

PRECIS

This system is dealt with here rather than immediately after chain indexing, as unlike the latter it is not dependent on a classification scheme for the derivation of its terms. It was developed because of the claim by its principal begetter, Derek Austin, and others working at BNB, that chain indexing could not be easily manipulated to produce by computer a series of subject terms related to a topic. This was because chain indexing at the BNB at that time (1970) was linked to DC, a scheme which created too many anomalies for a computer. It is also claimed that the PRECIS system developed naturally out of the work being done at that time by the Classification Research Group. Derek Langridge disputes this (Langridge 1976). Brian Vickery (Vickery 1975) and Langridge have both presented views about the validity of the system, but nevertheless it is well established as the method by which subject index entries are produced for BNB, having been used for this since 1971. A large manual of practice is available (Austin 1974) and there is a rapidly growing literature of explanation and comment. It seems likely that at some point in the not too distant future it will be adopted for use in BCM.

There is the further point that not everyone was happy with chain indexing as a method. It works very well with a faceted scheme such as BCM, but only the first entry is specific and some of the more general entries may direct users to class numbers which are part of the chain leading to a specific subject, but which themselves have no entries under them in a given issue of BCM or in a particular library's class catalogue. The index to BCM has no entry under *String quartets* as such; this is a highly sought term which chain procedure does not reveal. There is an entry under *String ensembles*, but the chain of the classification is used to take an enquirer from RW to RXNS. *Quartets : String ensemble* does lead directly to RXNS. A C Foskett (Foskett 1977 p 225) suggests four requirements for an alphabetical index system to replace chain indexing:

1. The heading must be coextensive with the subject at all access points.
2. It must not be geared to any particular classification scheme.
3. Each entry should be meaningful to the user, preferably without need for explanation.
4. The original indexing was to be intellectual, but all subsequent operations, including the generation of all entries and their filing, were to be done by computer.

He then proceeds to explain the PRECIS system so clearly (Foskett 1977 Chapter 14), there is little point in repeating it here and readers are referred to his account if a full explanation is required. The real virtue of the system lies in the second and fourth points of those enumerated above. However, the defects of the system, which evidence of use in BNB suggest, are firstly that the number of entries for any given subject is much higher than the corresponding number produced when using chain procedure, thus bulking the catalogue, increasing costs of production and possibly confusing readers with the proliferation of entries; secondly, that the strings of terms are not always produced as systematically in practice as the manual in theory suggests; thirdly, that too heavy a reliance is placed on cross references to cover defects in the basic system. The staff at the Bibliographical Services Division of the British Library produced by PRECIS a number of test indexes to issues of BCM (1973 to 75) for the Music Bibliography Group. Not all members of the group, nor indeed all members of the British Library staff involved, were satisfied with the result, and the advantage over the published BCM indexes, developed by chain procedure, was not immediately apparent. The difference between BCM and BNB is that the former uses a fully faceted scheme which produces a chain index automatically and is therefore perfectly capable of being manipulated by a computer.

While no statement has been made, British Library policy seems to be to replace the BCM scheme by Phoenix 780 and to change to PRECIS from chain procedure. It seems a short sighted policy to stop using a classification scheme of real distinction and merit together with an excellent indexing system which is proven and can be used easily by the lay person, in order to introduce a classification scheme of doubtful parentage (Phoenix 780) and an indexing system which appears to be no more effective than the one it is to replace.

An indication of how PRECIS would work with music can be gained by an examination of the treatment of the literature of music in BNB. A book on early percussion instruments receives the following entries in the subject index:

1 Percussion instrument playing.Performance.Early music 789'.01'0714

2 Percussion instruments
ca 1100 – ca 1650 789'.01'0902

3 Music
Early music.Performance.Percussion instruments playing. 789'.01'0714

4 Musical instrument playing
See also
Percussion instrument playing

5 Instruments, musical
See
Musical instruments

6 Musical instruments
See also
Percussion instruments

The first and third are indexed to the most specific class number. The second to an alternative placing, the two entries standing next to one another. They could of course be separated in a five year cumulation.

In the same year, a book on making early percussion instruments is indexed:

1 Percussion instruments
Early percussion instruments. Making – *Manuals* 789'.012

2 Musical instruments
Making – *manuals* 781.9'1

plus entries 5 and 6 for the first example.

Entries 1 and 3 for the first example demonstrate the process of 'shunting' which the computer carries out on the basic 'string' once this has been compiled. But why no entry under *Early music*? This is surely a recognized term. Readers who start under *instruments* have quite a journey round the bibliography. Readers who miss the reference under *musical instruments* and go straight to entry 2 for the second title may miss it altogether, as they are directed to a different class number which has no entry or reference. Why put the first book under two adjacent classes and make no link between two widely separated classes for the second book? If PRECIS is not linked to the classification, as is claimed, this ought not to happen and the connections would be made. This item was chosen at random and not deliberately selected. Readers are recommended to make similar investigations.

A book on the tenor sax player John Coltrane classed at 788'.66'0 924 receives the following entries in the subject index and shows more clearly the shunting process:

1 Jazz
  Performance. Saxophone playing. Coltrane, John –
  Biographies 788'.66'0924
2 Saxophone playing. Performance. Jazz
  Coltrane, John – *Biographies* 788'.66'0924
3 Coltrane, John. Saxophone playing. Performance. Jazz
  – *Biographies* 788'.66'0924
4 Biographies
  See also
    Biographies under names of specific subjects and persons.

Post-coordinate indexing

The methods so far described come under the general name of pre-coordinate indexing. This simply means that the work of producing compound subject or form terms has been carried out before an enquiry. With post-coordinate indexing the combination is devized at the time of the enquiry. In theory this should obviously allow for greater flexibility. So many different methods have been given this name that it is perhaps invidious to select two and describe them under the general heading of post-coordinate indexing. Nevertheless in dealing with a small collection these systems can be used to answer a wide variety of questions very effectively.

One system requires the use of edge-punched cards. As an item is added to a library employing this method, a card is completed with full bibliographical details and the classification symbol under which the item is shelved or filed. Subjects or forms are coded to the holes on the edge of the card. Thus the holes along one edge may represent medium of performance, while along another they may represent forms in music. Every time a piano sonata is added to stock, the holes representing the two terms *piano* and *sonata* are punched out of the card for the item, so that when a thin rod is passed through these holes the cards representing piano and sonata will fall from the file. The process can be repeated along the other two sides of the card for additional sought terms as necessary. This method has the advantage that it allows arrangement of the material on the shelves, and there is no limit to the number of items which can be coded in this way. It also has the advantage that the cards can be arranged in a convenient order eg by composer.

The second method is not so versatile. As each item is received it is given a number in succession. A card is made out for each term covered in the item and the number of the item recorded on each card. Thus after a number of documents have been received, there will be a collection of cards, each bearing the name of a focus in music and the numbers of the items in which it is included. Therefore, anyone interested in sonatas has only to turn to the relevant card and there find the scores, the numbers of which are recorded on the card. If Mozart's piano sonatas are required, then the cards for 'Mozart', 'piano' and 'sonatas' must be collated. The numbers common to all three cards will reveal the relevant scores. A sample check of such a system might show this:

Scores:

1 Mozart's piano sonata no 1
2 Beethoven piano concerto no 3
3 Brahm's clarinet sonata no 1 [clarinet and piano]
4 Hindemith's clarinet concerto
5 Mozart's piano concerto no 21.

Cards:

Mozart 1. 5.	Clarinet 3. 4
Piano 1. 2.3.5.	Beethoven 2
Sonata 1. 3.	Brahms 3
Concerto 2. 4. 5.	Hindemith 4

To use this sample to find a clarinet sonata, the cards reveal scores 3 and 4 for clarinet and 1 and 3 for sonata. The relevant score would be no 3–Brahm's clarinet sonata. A search for Mozart's piano music would reveal scores 1 and 5 to be applicable. Limit this to concertos and only no 5 is suitable.

The main disadvantage to this method is that the scores themselves cannot be arranged in any helpful order without some complication to the numbering, such as using the first three letters of the composer's name before each number to enable the scores to be arranged by composer. Thus the Mozart scores would be numbered successively as added MOZ 1, MOZ 2 etc. It also presupposes use of the catalogue for all searches, and obviously when the collection is large the whole method becomes too complicated. Nevertheless, it is simple to compile and it does reveal a lot of information quickly. It could be used very effectively for a small collection of material where it is not convenient for the reader to handle the scores. It is obviously very suitable for a closed-access recorded sound library.

APPENDICES

Appendix 1

Examples of cataloguing entries in accordance with AACR 2

These examples are not intended so much to cover problems as to demonstrate the layout of entries when rule 1.0D3 (Third level of description) is applied. Items 2, 4 and 5 show slightly different formats for entry under title proper.

1 **Britten. Concerto for piano and orchestra** (see p 66)

Britten, Benjamin

[Concertos, piano, orchestra, op.13]

Concerto for piano and orchestra op.13 [music] / Benjamin Britten. – London : Boosey & Hawkes, 1967.

1 miniature score (178p) ; 32 cm. – (Hawkes pocket scores)

Duration : 33 min. – Pl.no. : B & H 19511

or

Britten, Benjamin

[Concertos, piano, orchestra, op.13]

Concerto for piano and orchestra op.13 [music] / Benjamin Britten. – London : Boosey & Hawkes, 1967. – 1 miniature score (178p) ; 32 cm. – (Hawkes pocket scores). – Duration : 33 min. – Pl.no. : B & H 19511.

[Note: The rules (eg rule 1.5A1) for description allow the alternative forms of layout as shown. Obviously the second saves space, an important consideration in printed catalogues. The form *Benjamin Britten* accords with rule 22.2A. The uniform title plural form concertos follows rule 25.27B which requires use of the plural unless the composer wrote only one work of that musical type. Britten wrote concertos for piano and violin, one for each instrument]

2 **Anne Cromwell's virginal book**

Anne Cromwell's virginal book, 1638 [music] / transcribed and edited by Howard Ferguson. – London : Oxford University Press, 1974. – 1 score (iv, 51p.) : 2 facsims. ; 32 cm. – Transcribed from MS 46,78/748 [date 1638] belonging to London museum but

ANNE CROMWELL'S VIRGINAL BOOK, 1638

transcribed and edited by

Howard Ferguson

Oxford University Press
MUSIC DEPARTMENT
LONDON · NEW YORK

THE MUSIC IN

THE FAIRY QUEEN

ENGLISH OPERA (1692)

The Drama adapted from
A Midsummer Night's Dream
by
SHAKESPEARE

The music by

HENRY PURCELL

EDITED BY ANTHONY LEWIS

VOCAL SCORE

NOVELLO & COMPANY LIMITED
Borough Green Sevenoaks Kent

Edition Schott No. 1519

DIE SÖHNE BACH

LES FILS DE BACH

Une collection de morceaux originaux pour Piano composés par les quatre fils de J. S. Bach revue et choisie par

THE SONS OF BACH

A collection of original piano pieces composed by the four sons of J. S. Bach selected and edited by

Eine Sammlung ausgewählter Original=Klavierwerke der vier Söhne Joh. Seb. Bachs herausgegeben

von

Willy Rehberg

★

B. SCHOTT'S SÖHNE
MAINZ: Weihergarten 5
Paris: Editions Max Eschig
48 Rue de Rome

SCHOTT & Co. Ltd.
London W. 1: 48 Great Marlborough Str.
New-York: 1 West 47th Street
Associated Music Publishers Inc.

Printed in Germany — Imprimé en Allemagne

on loan to Cromwell Museum, Huntingdon. – Contents : Prelude / [John Bull] – A psalm : 'York' – Mrs Villier's sport – Bessie Bell – Frog's galliard /[John Dowland, set by ?] – Mr Ward's masque / [?John Ward]

[Note: A uniform title has not been used as it seems unnecessary here, as it would be the same as the title proper. There are fifty items in the volume, which would make a long list of contents. Added entries would be made under the appropriate heading for Ferguson, London Museum and Cromwell Museum. A reference would be needed from Cromwell, Anne. Analytical entries could be made for the named composers.]

3 **The Fairy Queen.**

Purcell, Henry

[The fairy queen. Vocal score]

The music in The Fairy queen [music] : English opera (1692) / the music by Henry Purcell; the drama adapted from a midsummer night's dream by Shakespears. – vocal score / edited by Anthony Lewis. – Sevenoaks : Novello, 1966. – 1 vocal score (169p.) ; 24 cm.

[Note: Added entries should be made under the heading for Lewis and Midsummer night's dream. The repetition of *vocal score* in the editor's statement seems unavoidable, as according to the introduction it is the vocal score which has been edited. This would not be clear if the edition statement were omitted.]

4 **Die Söhne Bach**

Die Söhne Bach [music] = Les fils de Bach . . . = The sons of Bach . . . : Eine Sammlung ausgewählter Original = Klavierwerke / der vier Söhne Joh. Seb. Bachs ; herausgegeben von Willy Rehberg. – Mainz ; London : Schott, . . .

[Note: This kind of title page is fairly common for music. See also p 70). The rules allow a fair amount of latitude in organizing the information eg 1.1E3, 1.1F6, 1.1F11. This example has been given to illustrate this point. The two publishers are closely associated and it seems reasonable to give the imprint as shown following rule 1.4D2].

5 **A sound recording (disc : 12 inch stereo). Side 1 label : Music from Prague/Leopold Kozeluch/Piano concerto in D Major/ Felicja Blumental, piano/Prague New Chamber Orchestra/conducted by Alberto Zedda/ Side 2 label : Music from Prague/Franz Krommer /Clarinet concerto in E flat major/David Glazer, clarinet/ Württemberg Chamber Orchestra, Heilbronn/conducted by Jörg Faerber. Turnabout TV 34279S.**

Music from Prague [sound recording] Piano concerto in D major / Leopold Koželuch. Clarinet concerto in E flat major / Franz Krommer. – London : Turnabout, 1970. – 1 sound disc (ca. 50 min) : 33⅓ rpm, stereo, 12 in. – Performers : Felicja Blumental, piano ; Prague New Chamber Orchestra, Alberto Zedda, conductor. David Glazer, clarinet ; Württemberg Chamber Orchestra, Jorg Faerber, conductor. – Turnabout : TV 34279S.

[Note: This is entered in accordance with rule 21.23D. For discs lacking a collective title it appears to be possible to treat each work separately under 6.1G. However, there seems to be no such provision for such items as this. See comment p 100. Assuming that rule 6.1G4, in spite of its being part of 6.1G **items without a collective title,** does also refer to items with a collective title (or could be made to refer) the entry for the first work on this disc would be:]

Koželuch, Leopold

[Concertos, piano, no.7, D major]

Piano concerto in D major [sound recording] Leopold Koželuch. – London : Turnabout, 1970. – on 1 side of 1 sound disc (ca. 25 min.) : 33⅓ rpm, stereo, 12 in. – Felicja Blumental, piano ; Prague New Chamber Orchestra. Alberto Zedda, conductor. – Turnabout : TV 34279S. – *With* : Krommer, Frantisek. Concertos, clarinet, no.1, E major.

[Note: I have used the Czech forms of the composers' names rather than the German forms in the headings].

6 **The physics of music.**

Wood, Alexander

The physics of music / by Alexander Wood. – 6th ed. / revised by J M Bowsher. – London : Methuen, 1962. xii, 258p., 16p. of plates : ill. ; 21cm. – (University paperbacks). – 1st ed. published : London : Methuen, 1944. – Bibliography : p 252.

ADDED ENTRIES (as First level of description 1.0D1 *but* omitting Extent of item and Notes.)

1 Bowsher, J M

Wood, Alexander

The physics of music. – 6th ed. / revised by J M Bowsher. – Methuen, 1962.

2 The Physics of music

Wood, Alexander

The physics of music. – 6th ed. / revised by J M Bowsher. – Methuen, 1962.

[Note: This item has been included to demonstrate treatment of monographs (eg no general material designation required: rule 1.1C1) and to show a possible layout for added entries, which have been abbreviated by omitting the last three items prescribed by the First level of description (as indicated above) but Bowsher's name (First statement of responsibility relating to the edition) has been retained in order to make clear the reason for the added entry under his name. *See 21.29F*]

Appendix 2

Specification of instrumentation

Union catalogue of orchestral scores and parts (IAML. UK)

[This system is suggested for small and medium sized libraries, especially those providing a service to amateur orchestras. It is taken from the introduction to the Catalogue. In a full catalogue entry this information is best supplied in the notes. In a short entry it could form part of the collation]

The orchestration is expressed as follows:

1 *The basic instruments* (wood-wind, brass, timpani, percussion, keyboard, strings) are presented in conventional score order. Wood-wind and brass are indicated by two blocks of four numbers (or zeros) representing respectively (i) flutes, oboes, clarinets, bassoons. (ii) horns, trumpets, trombones, tubas. The number of instruments is always indicated by a figure in the same position eg 2222 4231 always means double wood-wind and standard brass of 4 horns, 2 trumpets, 3 trombones, tuba. Auxiliary instruments used frequently eg piccolo, cor anglais, bass clarinet and contra bassoon are indicated by the presence of an asterisk preceding the number of instruments in that column.

(N.B. The system does not differentiate between doubling or additional auxiliary instruments ie *2 *200 could mean 2 flutes doubling piccolo or 1 flute plus piccolo, 2 oboes doubling cor anglais, or 1 oboe plus 1 cor anglais).

Other additional and auxiliary instruments follow the main sequence of instruments after strings, eg *3222 4231 T.PERC.CEL.HP. STR.SAX.EUPH.

2 Timpani, percussion and keyboard are between brass and strings. The abbreviation 'PERC' indicates the presence of any standard untuned percussion instruments, eg tambourine, triangle, bass drum etc; keyboard and harp follow this sequence.

3 Strings follow percussion and keyboard indicated by the abbreviation STR.

4 Additional instruments follow strings. These are any other auxiliary and additional wood-wind or brass such as saxophones, euphoniums, serpents, etc continuo.

5 Solo instruments *not* specified in the title follow additional instruments but are preceded by a colon.

6 Voices (both chorus and soli) follow solo instruments also preceded by a colon. ('Chorus' means SATB chorus, all other are specified).
N.B. Any or all of these "fields" may be present.

Examples of possible orchestrations:

i) *3*322 4231 T.PERC.CEL.XYL.HP.STR.2SAX: SOLO VLA: CHORUS, SOLO SATB.

ii) 0200 2000 T.PERC.STR.CONT: CHORUS.

iii) HP.STR.

iv) STR.

Optional instruments are indicated by round brackets (HP).

BBC Catalogue of Orchestral music

[This system is suggested for libraries with a large collection of orchestral music]

The instruments are shown in groups following conventional score order, separated by oblique strokes, as follows:
woodwind/brass/percussion/keyboard & miscellaneous/strings/continuo/voices

In the case of the woodwind and brass sections, the number of instruments is shown by groups of figures, eg 2232/4231, indicating the numbers of players required for flutes, oboes, clarinets, bassoons, horns, trumpets, trombones, and tuba respectively.

Auxiliary instruments are shown after the appropriate main instrument, according to the following system:

a) If a separate player is required, a 'plus' sign (+) is used, eg 2.2+ca.22 means that a separate cor anglais player is required, in addition to the two oboists.

b) Instruments doubled by existing players are shown in round brackets. Within these brackets, the number of players who double is shown together with the appropriate abbreviation eg 3(2picc)333 indicates triple woodwind in which two of the flute players double piccolo. If a player doubles more than one instrument, a comma is used, eg 3(afl,bfl)333 shows that one of the flautists doubles both alto and bass flutes. A colon is used, to separate instruments within the brackets which are doubled by different players, eg 3(2 picc: afl, bfl)333 shows that two of the flautists double piccolo, while the third doubles both alto and bass flutes.

Additional instruments are inserted into sequences by the use of full-stops, eg 322.2asx.2 shows that two alto saxophones are required in addition to three flutes, two oboes, two clarinets and two bassoons. (See 'Order of citation for wind instruments' for the relevant place in the sequence)

Alternative instruments are shown by the means of an 'equals' sign (=) in square brackets: eg org[=pf] means organ or piano. This is also used to indicate reduced instrumentation, eg 333[=2]33 means that two oboes may be used instead of three, if desired. Square brackets are also used to indicate optional instruments, eg cel.[gtr]hp.pf, and in combination with the 'plus' sign (+) to show optional additional numbers of instruments, eg 1[+].111 indicates one or more flutes. Where there are no wind instruments, the layout is presented as follows: hp/str perc/hp/str

Order of citation for wind instruments

Additional and auxiliary instruments should follow the main instruments in the following order:

FLUTES

auxiliary : piccolo, alto flute, recorders (sirec.drec.tblrec.brec.gbrec)

OBOES

auxiliary : oboe da caccia, oboe d'amore, cor anglais, bass oboe

additional : heckelphone, shawm [crumhorn unless score indicates elsewhere]

CLARINETS

auxiliary : E♭ clarinet, alto clarinet, bass clarinet

additional : bassethorn, heckelclarina, saxophones.

BASSOONS

auxiliary : contra-bassoons

additional : sarrusaphone (and serpent if the score indicates this to be the most suitable place).

HORNS

auxiliary : corno da caccia

additional : Wagner tuba

TRUMPETS

auxiliary : sopranino (or piccolo) tpts.Ftpt.E♭tpt.Dtpt. basstpt (in C). B♭tpt.

additional : bugle, flugelhorns, saxhorns, cornet, althorn, cornetts.

TROMBONES (where 3 trombones are listed they are taken to be 2 tenor and 1 brass).

auxiliary : bass trombone, contra-bass trombone

additional : sackbuts

TUBA

auxiliary : Tenor tuba, E♭ Bass tuba, BB♭ Bass tuba.

additional : baritone, euphonium, ophicleide, serpent (or after woodwind if more suitable)

Auxiliary and additional instruments are inserted into the main sequence in the following order:

a) Woodwind: fl.picc.afl.bfl.sirec.drec.tblrec.trec.brec.gbrec. ob.ob-dc.ob-d'a.ca.bob.heck[cmhn]. shm.cl.A♭cl.E♭cl.Dcl.acl.bcl.cbc.bthn.sisx.ss. asx.tsx.barsx.cbsn.[sarr] [spt]

b) Horns and Brass: hn.wtuba. twtuba. tpt.ptpt.Ftpt.E♭tpt. Dtpt.Ftpt.E♭cnt.cnt.flg.cntto.tbn.atbn.atbn. vtbn.btbn. tuba.ttuba.E♭tuba.BB♭tuba.bar.euph.oph.[sarr] [spt]

Percussion The abbreviation 'perc' indicates the more usual percusion instruments to be found in orchestral music, such as cymbals, bass drum, triangle, etc, without specifying the number of players. If only one player is specified, this is shown as '1 perc'; two players as '2 perc', etc. However, the number of players required for the percussion instruments is often not specified in scores, in which case the instruments are simply listed by their abbreviations, eg perc. bell,glock.tamtam,xyl. If the players for each instrument are in fact specified, the system described above is used, eg timp.2 perc (bells: tamtam)+glock(vib) means a timpanist, two players on basic instruments (one of whom doubles tubular bells, the other doubling tamtam) and a separate glockenspiel player doubling vibraphone.

If the total number of percussion players is given, without specifying which instrument is played by whom, the abbreviation are enclosed within round brackets, eg timp.3perc(bells.vib.xyl) indicates a timpanist and three percussion players who cover basic instruments, tubular bells, vibraphone and xylophone between them. A number preceding the abbreviation 'timp' refer to the number of players, rather than the number of drums.

Keyboard & miscellaneous are arranged in alphabetical order, including: acc.bjo.cel.cim.cta.dulc.egtr.eorg.epf.gtr.hca.hmn.hp. hpsd.jpf.mand.om.org.pf.prpf.syn.tbjo.

Strings The abbreviation 'str' may be qualified by the addition of information in brackets, eg 'str (no vlns)' or the abbreviation 'str' may be omitted if there are only a few instruments eg 2222/2100/ vlc. cb. Where the exact number of instruments is specified, the following forms should be used: 'str (8.6.4.2.1)'. If the violins are not divided into firsts and seconds, the form 'str (24.-.8.6.4)' is used. Single instruments are shown as 'str (1.-.1.1.0)', but in general the shortest method is used, eg '3 vlc' rather than 'str (0.-.0.3.0)'. If the number of desks is specified in the score, this is converted into the number of players for the catalogue entry.

Continuo The following methods are used:

a) figured bass (no instruments specified)–cont
b) instruments specified by composer or editor–cont (hpsd.bsn)
c) realised by someone other than the editor (no instruments specified)–cont (real.R.P.Block)
d) instruments specified by realiser–cont (org.vlc: real.A.Schönberg)

If a keyboard instrument apart from the continuo part is called for, this is listed in the usual keyboard & miscellaneous section.

The abbreviation 'cont' indicates that a continuo is present; the bass instrument, whether bassoon or cello, often being included in the list of instruments, although such specification of continuo instruments is frequently editorial rather than original.

Electronics If the work involves a pre-recorded tape or disc, or involves electronic equipment (other than synthesizers, which are listed in the keyboard section), this is shown after the strings. The abbreviation 'elec' covers all electronic equipment except synthesizers.

Voices are given at the end of the instrumentation if they have not already been mentioned in the title, except in the case of operattas, operas, musical plays, etc eg 2222/4231/timp/str/SMzBar-soli. mv-chorus. Chorus means SATB chorus unless otherwise specified.

Alternative versions are in the form:

2122/4331/timp/str [or 1111/1100/str]

In the case of a 'concert' orchestra, the rhythm section is listed between the brass and the percussion. Include the rhythm section in the title eg FOXTROT for orchestra with rhythm section 222.3sx. 2/4321/rhythm-bgtr.kit/timp/str.

As an example of the system, the instrumentation of a work for a large orchestra might be shown as follows:

2(pic)+afl.2+ca.3(E♭cl:bcl)2.+cbsn/4331.euph/2timp.perc. glock.xyl/gtr(mand).hp.org[=pf] /str(24.-.10.8.6)S-solo mv-chorus

which indicates two flutes (one of which doubles piccolo), with a separate player on alto flute, two oboes with a separate player on cor anglais, three clarinets, with one doubling E♭cl and another doubling bass cl, two bassoons with a separate player on contra-bassoon; four horns, three trumpets, three trombones, tuba, euph-onium; timpani (2 players), basic percussion, glockenspiel and xylophone (number of players not specified); guitar (doubling mandoline), harp, organ or piano; strings: twenty-four violins (not divided into Firsts and Seconds), ten violas, eight cellos and six basses; a soprano soloist and a male voice chorus.

Small orchestra

Where no wind instruments are present the entire wind code is omitted, eg hp/str, but where instruments are present in one area only, eg either wind or brass, zeros are inserted elsewhere, eg 0000/4231/str

In the case of early works, the abbreviation 'str' sometimes covers the specification of viols; the parts being playable by a modern string orchestra.

Works with solo instruments/voices

Where a work has solo instruments/voices mentioned in the title, these are not repeated in the orchestration. eg Concerto for piano & orch.

2222/4230/str

[Note: When the BBC's Orchestral catalogue is published it will contain a full list of abbreviations. Those used in this extract are reasonably self explanatory. The abbreviations for wind instruments can be worked out from the list of names above them. Si = sop-ranino, S = soprano might be difficult to distinguish. In the section on voices Mz = mezzosoprano).]

Appendix 3

MARC Format

MARC stands for MAchine Readable Catalog. This is a system whereby a cataloguing agency, eg LC or BNB, produces machine readable catalogue data on magnetic tapes, which are made available to subscribing libraries. The latter then process the tapes through their own computer to produce, for example, catalogue cards. At a British seminar held in 1969 EHC Driver suggested that a better definition for MARC would be Multi Access Research Catalogue (*Seminar on the UK Marc project, Southampton, 1969. Proceedings* edited by A E Jeffreys and T D Wilson. Newcastle: Oriel Press for LA Cataloguing and Indexing Group, 1970. p.56). Certainly the range of library activities for which MARC can be used is potentially very wide: selection, ordering, production of bibliographies, information retrieval etc, any activity for which a printed national bibliography can be used. The process is infinitely quicker with a computer.

The Music Bibliography Group's MARC Format Subgroup has produced a MARC format for music, which is to appear publicly for the first time in an issue of *MARC news* in 1979 and be published separately by the British Library soon after. The American MARC format for music has already been published (*Music: A MARC format.* Library of Congress, MARC Development Office, 1976. available from the Superintendent of Documents, U.S. Government Printing Office, Washington DC, 20402). The use of MARC is spreading to many other countries outside the English speaking world eg France, Germany, the Netherlands, Scandinavia etc.

In its first report (1975) the Music Bibliography Group's Subgroup provided the following useful summary of the MARC process:

Format function can be summarised as providing the ability to

SELECT (and by converse REJECT)
MANIPULATE
and DISPLAY

on any of the defined record characteristics or data elements, in order, among other objectives, to permit EFFECTIVE INTERCHANGE.

The MARC format is a method of handling MAchine Readable Cataloguing information. It provides packages of information—a kit of parts, as it were, which users put together to suit their own requirements. The information package for each item is called the RECORD.

Data elements

For the computer to be able to manipulate it, the information has to be broken down into small, separately identifiable pieces, which are known as *data elements*. Some of these are codes (for example the country of publication), and some are recognisable parts of 'catalogue-entries-to-be' like an author's surname. The area of a record containing one or more data elements is a *field*. In the MARC format each field is labelled with a three-digit *tag*, which describes the information and its function. In addition to tags *indicators* and *subfield codes* are used. Indicators add to the definition of a particular field and supply information which generates a manipulative action.

Subfield codes identify the separate data elements present in a field which have retrieval value and which assist articulation in filing and output listing.

It also provided an example of a BCM entry in a MARC format, using the BLCMP's 'MARC format for music and sound recordings' and input proforma. The entry and proforma are reproduced here:

QPE

HODDINOTT, Alun
[Sonata for piano, no. 6. Op. 78, no. 3]
Sonata no.6. Opus 78, no.3/by
Alun Hoddinott. – London:
Oxford University Press, 1974.-15p;
4to.
Duration 10 min.
ISBN 0193728400: £1.25 (B74-50572)

It will be observed that this item has an ISBN. This should not be taken as typical of music publishing. It was one of the few music items in BCM for that year to have an ISBN.

The decision which must be made by individual libraries on whether to use MARC records is very much a question of management. Various

BLCMP MONOGRAPHS GENERAL DATA INPUT FORM FORM MON. C

Field	Code	Entry
Control number	M	0193728400
Change code: n = new; a = add; c = correct; d = delete	g	n
Date of publication	a	S1974bbbb
Country of publication code	b	uk
Intellectual level code	d	
Form of publication code	f	
Government publication designator	g	
Conference proceedings designator	h	
Literary text/type of publication code	l	
Biographical material code	m	
Main language code (LEAVE BLANK IF ENGLISH)	n	
Analytical record designator	y	
Type of record code	z	c

TAGS AND INDICATORS MUST BE COMPLETED AS REQUIRED AND SUBFIELD DELIMITERS AND CODES ENTERED

Languages	+041 0 *a +01500 *a b7450572
B.C.M. class	+085 *a QPE
M.I.C.	+086 *a
Author (1xx)	+1 0 0 1 0 *a Hoddinott *h Alun
Uniform title	+240 3 0 *c Sonata *d piano *e no.6 *f op.78 *g no.3
Collective title	+243 0 *a
Title	+245 0 0 *a Sonata no.6, opus 78, no.3 *d by Alun Hoddinott
Edition	+250 0 *a

Imprint	+260 0 0 *a London *b Oxford University Press *c 1974
Collation	+300 *a 15p *c 10cm +35000 *a £1.25
Series (4xx; 8xx)	+4 *a
Notes (5xx)	+5 0 0 0 0 *a Duration: 10 min
Subject headings (6xx)	+6 *a
Added entries (7xx)	+7 *a
Cross references (9xx)	+9 *a
End of record	+ N/L

Compiled Date	Checked Date	Punched Date	Verified Date

cost factors have to be considered, some of them not always easy to calculate. Research into the whole question of catalogue performance in terms of its ability to fulfill the needs of the user has been in process at Bath University since the early 1970's. Such investigation is a timely and useful reminder that the main function of a library's catalogue is to help readers to establish if the library in question has a particular item and, if it has, where that item can be found. The cost of not finding such information and also the kind of detail about the item, which a MARC record bears, has to be measured against the cost of supplying the catalogue entry in the first place.

Many libraries do not require the amount of detail in their entries which a MARC record provides. If MARC tapes are used the record may have to be adjusted to local needs. The need for adjustment depends on how many of the items purchased annually by a library are catalogued by the cataloguing agency providing the tapes. If the correlation is high, then it is probably cheaper if the cataloguing of items not in the MARC tapes is done locally to MARC standards.

Such considerations depend ultimately on the *coverage* MARC tapes provide of a library's acquisitions and the *currency* of the MARC record when one is available. As far as the currency is concerned this has always been a problem in using central cataloguing agencies and the failure of such organizations to provide an up to date service has caused much frustration. BLCMP'S coverage of music is probably the highest in the United Kingdom, simply because a number of music libraries participate in the scheme and contribute records of their accessions to the data bank.

An interesting example of the use of a MARC format for RISM, with discussion by Kurt Dorfmüller of the attendant problems, is to be found in *Fontes artis musicae* xxv, 1978/4.

Appendix 4

Examples of cataloguing entries of microform from the Pendlebury Library of Music

These examples were supplied by Richard Andrewes, the Librarian, and illustrate a number of points. They were of course catalogued before the publication of AACR 2 and therefore should not be studied as examples of layout according with the new code. Certain details, such as the location of the item in the Pendlebury Library, have been omitted as not relevant to their reproduction in this appendix.

Examples 1 to 3 are of microfilms of manuscripts or early printed editions supplied by libraries. The first two show the use of uniform titles and all three demonstrate clearly how to supply information about the supplying library, date of the manuscript or printing when known and date of the copy. Details of the microform are clearly supplied, as well as essential information about the manuscript.

Examples 4 and 5 are of microfilms supplied by a publisher.

Example 1

GREENE, Maurice

[While George provok'd to vengeance arms.]

Ode / composed by G.F. Handel. . .1740. – 1977
(Cambridge : University Library.)
1 microfilm reel (35 frames) : negative ; 35mm. – For STB soli, chorus and orchestra. – Composed by Maurice Greene ; words by Colley Cibber. – Original manuscript score, partly holograph, belongs to Richard Luckett, St. Catharine's College, Cambridge.

Example 2

CAVAZZONI, Girolamo

[Intavolatura, organ, book 2.]

Intabulatura d'organo : cioe misse, himni, magnificat. . .libro secondo / composti per Hieronimo de Marcantonio da Bologna, detto d'Urbino. – [196-] (Bologna : Civico Museo Bibliografico Musicale.)
1 microfilm reel (ca.40 frames) : negative ; 35mm. – Original keyboard score, published : Venice, [154-]. – Photo of copy in I Bc.

Example 3

LOVE in a village. – [196-?] (London : Royal College of Music)
1 microfilm reel (ca.150 frames ; positive) ; 35mm. – Music by Handel, Boyce, and others, selected and arranged by Arne. – The original ms. full score, written in the late 18th century, is in GB Lcm, ms. 342.

Example 4

CHRISTCHURCH, Oxford. *Library*. Ms.Mus.21.
[A collection of vocal and instrumental music.] – [1976] (Cambridge; Cambridge Microfilms.)
1 microfilm reel (192 frames) : positive ; 35mm. – Photo of manuscript score, English, 17th century.

Example 5

ANDERSON, Ronald Eugene
Richard Alison's Psalter (1599) and devotional music in England to 1640 / Ronald Eugene Anderson. – Ann Arbor : University Microfilms, 1974.
1 microfilm reel (frames ; positive) ; 35mm. – PhD thesis, University of Iowa, 1974. – Includes an edition of music, p.441-646. – Bibliography: p.647-669.

Bibliography and References

The hope was expressed in volume one that this second volume might contain a comprehensive bibliography. In fact pressures of other work and the need to keep the cost within reasonable bounds have prevented this. The works cited in the following are those which I have found useful and/or interesting. In any case too long a bibliography can prove a daunting prospect for readers.

The practice in volume one of indicating with an asterisk those works which themselves have significant bibliographies has been repeated here, except where the title makes it obvious.

References in the text of this volume are by author's name and date of the item eg Austin 1974 (p 111) clearly refers to the second item listed under Derek Austin, as the content indicates that the reference is to the manual. Coates 1960 (p 103) refers to Coates, E J. Subject catalogues London, Library Association, 1960. Bibliographical details of the codes and standards are given in the introduction.

Items listed in volume one, apart from the periodicals, have not been repeated here unless they have been referred to in the text.

Periodicals

Brio
Catalogue & index
Fontes artis musicae
Library resources and technical services
Music cataloging bulletin
Notes

Abstracts

Library and information science abstracts (LISA)
Répertoire internationale de littérature musicale (RILM)

Bibliography and references

*Austin, Derek. 'The development of PRECIS: a theoretical and technical history'. *Journal of documentation* 30(1), March 1974, 47-102.

Austin, Derek. *PRECIS: a manual of concept analysis and subject indexing*. London, BNB, 1974.
*Bradley, Carol June *editor. Reader in musical librarianship*. Washington, Microcard Edition Books, 1973.
Brook, Barry S. *Thematic catalogues in music: an annotated bibliography*. New York, Pendragon Press, 1972.
Brophy, Peter. 'The management of cataloguing'. *Library management news* 5, August 1978, 9-15. An excellent analysis. Further comment by D E Lewis appears in no 7, February 1979, 21-23.
Coates, E J. *Subject catalogues: headings and structure*. London. Library Association, 1960.
*Coral, Lenore. 'The historical development of the thematic catalogue'. Bradley, Carol June. *Reader in music librarianship* q.v. 185-192.
Cutter, Charles A. *Rules for a dictionary catalog*. Washington: Government Printing Office, 1904; London, Library Association, 1935.
Elmer, Minnie. 'Classification, cataloguing, indexing'. Bradley, Carol June. *Reader in music librarianship* q.v. 148-155. Reprinted from *Notes: supplement for members* 25, December 1957, 23-28.
Ferris, Dave. 'The LANCET cataloguing rules: reflections after a year'. *Audiovisual librarian* 2(1), Spring 1975, 16-23.
Foreman, Lewis. *Discographies: a bibliography*. London, Triad Press, 1973.
*Foreman, Lewis. *Systematic discography*. London, Bingley; Hamden, Conn, Linnet; 1974.
*Foskett, A C. *The subject approach to information*. 3rd ed. London, Bingley; Hamden, Linnet Books, 1977.
Gray, Michael H & Gibson, Gerald D. *Bibliography of discographies. Vol 1. Classical music, 1925-1975*. New York, London, Bowker, 1977.
Heyer, Anna Harriet. *Historical sets, collected editions, and monuments of music: a guide to their contents*. 2nd ed. Chicago, American Library Association, 1969. (*See* also Charles, Sidney Robinson. *A handbook of music literature* in *sets and series*. New York: Free Press, 1972).
*Horner, John. *Special cataloguing.* London, Bingley; Hamden, Conn, Linnet; 1973.
*Hunter, Eric J. *Cataloguing: a guidebook.* London, Bingley; Hamden, Conn, Linnet; 1974.
Johansson, Carl. 'The new numericode thematic catalogue in the

Library of the Royal Swedish Academy of Music in Stockholm'. *Fontes artis musicae* XXV, 1978/1, 52-56.

*Jones, Malcolm. *Music librarianship*. London, Bingley, 1979.

Jones, Malcolm. 'Printed music and the MARC format'. *Program* 10(4) October 1976, 119-122.

Kaufman, Judith. *Recordings of non-western music: subject and added entry access.* Music Library Association technical reports no 5, 1977.

Langridge, Derek. Review of Derek Austin's *PRECIS: a manual* q.v. *Journal of librarianship* 8(3), July 1976, 210-212.

Library of Congress. *Subject headings* 8th ed. Washington, 1975.

Samuel, Harold E. 'Musicology and the music library'. *Library trends* 25(4), April 1977, 833-846.

Schiødt, Nanna. 'MUSICAT. A method of cataloguing music manuscripts by computer as applied in the Danish RISM manuscript project'. *Fontes artis musicae* XXIII, 1976/4, 158-167.

Sears list of subject headings. 10th ed.; Edited by Barbara M. Westby. New York, H W Wilson, 1972.

UK MARC manual. First standard edition. London: British Library Bibliographical Services Division. 1975.

*Watanabe, Ruth T. *Introduction to music research.* Englewood Cliffs, N J, Prentice Hall, 1967.

Vickery, B C. Review of Derek Austin's *PRECIS: a manual* q.v. *Catalogue & index* 38, Autumn 1975, 10-11.

*Woakes, Harriet Coleman. *Classification and cataloguing in ethnomusicology*. Dissertation. London, University College, 1978. Unpublished.

Early music catalogues

The major project to examine here is RISM (Munich, Henle; Kassel, Barenreiter, 1960-). It is published in two series:

Series	A	Alphabetical
	A/1	Music printed between 1500 and 1800.
	A/2	Pre 1800 manuscripts
Series	B	Type of format

See also the very useful example of a detailed catalogue of early music manuscripts produced by computer as a part of the RISM project which occupies almost the whole of *Fontes artis musicae* XXV, 1978/4.

Four other catalogues which illustrate different styles are:

The British union-catalogue of early music printed before the year 1801. Edited by Edith B Schnapper. London, Butterworth, 1957. 2 vols.

Catalogue of manuscript music in the British Museum. Edited by Augustus Hughes-Hughes. London, British Museum, 1906-1909. 3 vols. (*Handlist of music manuscripts acquired 1908-1967.* Edited by Pamela J Willetts. London British Museum. 1970).
These are not limited to early music, but contain many examples of the practice of one of the greatest music libraries in the world.

Duckles, Vincent *and others. Thematic catalog of a manuscript collection of eighteenth century Italian instrumental music in the University of California, Berkeley, Music Library.* Berkeley: University of California Press, 1963.
Meyer-Baer, Kathi. *Liturgical music incunabula: a descriptive catalogue.* London: Bibliographical Society, 1962.

INDEX TO CODE RULES

This refers to comment made on individual rules.
Reference is by rule number for AACR 1 and 2, IAML 2 and 3, by topic for IAML.1, 4 and 5.
For ISBD's refer to general index.

GENERAL INDEX

The terms *music* and *cataloguing* have only been used as qualifiers in this index, when essential to make the reason for the entry clear. For AACR and IAML rules see the Index to code rules.